EVERYTHING ABOUT HIM

Patricia Lynn

ZEBRA BOOKS
KENSINGTON PUBLISHING CORP.

ZEBRA BOOKS are published by

Kensington Publishing Corp.
850 Third Avenue
New York, NY 10022

First Zebra Printing: May, 1996
10 9 8 7 6 5 4 3 2 1

Printed in the United States of America

One

Amy Michaels hurried along the nearly deserted Indianapolis International Airport terminal. She made an awkward attempt to juggle her carry-on case and her oversized purse, while trying to catch a glimpse of her watch. It was a useless maneuver. She sighed and kept moving, trying to force a little more speed out of her overworked and protesting legs. At least it would be easy to find her suitcase at the luggage area. Everyone else should be gone by now.

She rounded a corner and came to the slowly rotating conveyor belt. After setting her case and purse on the floor at her feet, she stretched her aching shoulders, and made a silent vow to buy a backpack.

She watched, willing her suitcase to appear. With a sigh, she eased first one foot and then the other out of her black dress pumps. After twelve hours of work and two hours on an airplane, the shoes felt like they'd shrunk a size or two. She smoothed a hand down the skirt of her gray shirtdress in an attempt to erase the wrinkles. It did no good. She would have to look as frazzled as she felt.

She focused her attention back on the conveyor belt, which had creaked to a stop. It was empty. She fought back the impulse to throw herself onto it and sob.

Amy took a deep breath and decided not to panic. At least not yet. She quickly scanned the area, wondering if someone might have picked up her suitcase by mistake. It didn't seem possible, given its unique color. Maybe the airline had lost it. She immediately pushed that thought away, not even wanting to consider that kind of problem. Perhaps someone stole it.

Turning, she looked down the long, empty corridor, and a splash of familiar color caught her eye. A man stood at a bank of pay phones, his back to her and her suitcase at his feet. She was positive it was hers. In all of the trips she'd made, she had never seen another bright orange suitcase like that one. It was always easy to spot when thrown in with all the other luggage of the world.

Silently fuming, she picked up her things and marched purposely forward. What kind of idiot would take a suitcase as ugly as hers? This guy must be color blind.

As she approached, she took inventory of the unsuspecting culprit. His sandy hair was thick and neatly cut at the collar of his casual knit shirt. The solid red fabric stretched over broad shoulders and disappeared into the waistband of well-worn jeans. Those jeans molded lean hips and thighs and long legs.

She decided to be polite. After all, he might have a logical explanation. If he'd meant to steal her suitcase, he wouldn't have stopped to make a phone call.

The man reached up with his left hand and rubbed the back of his neck. There was no ring on his finger. Amy's interest was piqued. Maybe he wasn't married. Not that the absence of a ring guaranteed that he was single. She'd found that out firsthand a year ago. A painful, but well-learned lesson.

He replaced the receiver, and she stepped forward. "Excuse me," she said firmly. "That's my suitcase you've got there."

Slowly, he turned and she found herself under the scrutiny of very blue eyes. She paled, and then, almost instantly, blushed.

He arched an eyebrow and crossed his arms against his

chest. "Lady, are you sure you want this thing?" Familiar merriment sparkled in his eyes. "It's really ugly."

Amy had to laugh. "Hey, don't criticize my luggage." She tried to sound sufficiently insulted but couldn't pull it off. "What are you doing here, Joel? I thought my dad was going to pick me up."

"Change in plans. Didn't Susan tell you?"

Amy shook her head. "She must have forgotten."

"Figures. Her mind's on her wedding, and nothing else matters."

"Good thing you're handling the minor details. Like picking up the maid of honor."

He gave an exaggerated sigh. "One more week, then I gladly give up all responsibility."

"Spoken like a loving big brother," Amy noted wryly, not believing for a minute that his complaints were genuine.

She looked up into Joel Hartman's familiar face and felt a strange quickening of her pulse. Why hadn't she recognized him immediately? His eyes were still as blue as a cloudless summer day and his hair, a cross between brown and blond, still fell stubbornly across his forehead. As always, she resisted the urge to reach up and brush it back.

His features were still strong and lean, a shadow of beard covering his jaw, a faint scar marring his firm chin. She remembered that she'd been the cause of that. He'd been helping her climb over a fence, and her foot had slipped. In an effort to keep her from falling, he'd cut his chin against a piece of sharp metal. It was just one of the many times over the years that Joel Hartman had come to her rescue.

She smiled. What a hoot! Her best friend's older brother, her childhood hero, and she had taken him for a thief.

Joel smiled back, and bent to pick up her suitcase.

"I'll take that," he offered, reaching for her carry-on, too. "Come on. Car's this way."

He turned and started off down the corridor. For a moment Amy lagged behind, admiring his easy stride. Why had she never noticed how good he looked in snug denims?

Mentally, she smacked herself and picked up her pace. For heaven's sake! She'd known Joel her whole life, but she'd never thought of him as sexy, if that was the right word. He glanced over his shoulder and grinned at her. It was the right word.

"Better get a move on," he said. "Your parents are going to wonder what's happened to you."

She hurried to catch up.

He pushed through the glass doors leading into the parking garage, and she came to a dead halt. Something very strange was happening here. A faint tingling danced down her spine. Exactly when had Joel acquired that sexy smile?

Firmly pushing the feeling and the uncomfortable thoughts aside, she found herself once again hurrying to catch up with him. Her legs had to work double time to match his long steps. When they came to a halt at a sleek, black sports car, she was actually out of breath.

He popped the hatchback and stowed her suitcase inside, then reached for the rest of her luggage. The irresistible scent of a brand-new car drifted on the air, and Amy inhaled deeply.

"Wow. The real estate business must be pretty good if you can afford to drive this," she observed, her voice filled with awe. "I'm definitely in the wrong line of work."

He closed the hatchback and walked around to her side of the car. With his thumb he pressed a remote on his key chain, releasing the automatic door locks. "Business is good." He pulled the door open for her. "But this isn't my car."

Joel helped her in and shut the door carefully. Amy looked out, her face framed for a moment by the pale green glass of the window. A riot of dark curls skimmed her shoulders and she brushed them back from her face. Amber eyes, framed with dark, spiky lashes, gazed up at him, bright with interest. Her nose was straight, tilted slightly upward on the end, and her chin was as stubborn as he remembered. There was a healthy glow to her skin and a half smile curving her full lips.

He'd always considered her cute in a wholesome sort of way. Looking at her now, he realized he needed to revise his opinion. Amy was hovering just on the edge of beautiful. Somehow he had missed the transition. Until now.

The unexpected direction of his thoughts momentarily stunned him. Bemused, he reminded himself that she was just Amy. There was nothing mysterious or alluring about her. For the twenty-six years of her life, she'd been either a joy or a pain to him. Just like his sister Susan.

Shaking off the strange awareness, he walked around to the driver's side and slid inside. He turned the ignition key, and the engine purred to life immediately.

Amy sank back into the rich burgundy leather with an appreciative sigh and looked around the luxurious interior. There was a console loaded with buttons for power everything, and a state-of-the-art stereo system.

"What kind of friend loans you a car like this?"

"A very close one."

Amy thought about his answer even as she became aware of a lingering feminine scent intermingled with the aroma of new leather. She cast him a sidelong glance as he smoothly merged into southbound interstate traffic.

"She must be pretty special," she said lightly.

He shrugged. "I guess she is."

Amy hesitated only a moment. "Is she The One?"

He looked at her then, briefly. Amazing how much annoyance one look could contain. She slid down a little further into the seat.

"Mind your own business, Amy. Okay?"

"Fine."

She sounded insulted and hurt at the same time, and Joel had to smile. Amy had never been good at hiding her feelings. If her expressive amber-colored eyes didn't give her away, her voice would. It was something he had learned about her early on. And over the years, occasionally, he hadn't been above using this knowledge to his benefit.

"All right," he said with a sigh. "Her name is Debra Marsh, and she's a pediatrician, with a very successful private practice. She's away this last week and left the car with me."

"She trusts you with a car like this? Must be love."

He laughed shortly. "No."

"Why not?"

He cast her a quick glance, a frown crinkling his forehead. "Why this sudden interest in my love life?"

Amy shook her head, as surprised by her question as he was. "Just asking. Didn't mean to be nosy. Sorry."

"It's okay." He was silent a long moment. "Anyway, I'm not in love."

An awkward pause compelled Amy to change the subject. "How are Susan and Brad?"

"Lovey-dovey as ever."

"I think they're perfect for each other. Don't you?"

"Yeah. They're going to be happy."

Amy heard the absolute certainty in his words and was pleased by it. Charles Hartman, Joel and Susan's father, had died suddenly nine years before. Joel had taken his new status as male head of the household very seriously. The job included seeing his sister through her last year of high school and four years of college. Amy knew that seeing Susan happily married would make Joel as proud as any father.

Joel had been a year old when his parents, Charles and Anne Hartman, had moved in next door to Neil and Brenda Michaels. The two couples had become close friends. Susan and Amy had been born five years later, only weeks apart. They grew up as close as sisters and Joel naturally became a traditional big brother to both of them.

"Well, what about you?" Joel broke into her thoughts. "Is there someone special in your life?"

She felt a slight twinge of regret, but ignored it. "Nope. No one."

"What happened to that architect you were dating? Susan seemed to think it was pretty serious."

"It wasn't," she answered simply, wanting to avoid the details. "How's your business doing?"

He recognized the deliberate change in topic and let it stand. "It's doing great. I've got some super agents and the real estate market is picking up."

"I'd like to buy a house," Amy said reflectively. "But with all the traveling I do, it wouldn't make sense."

"How is your job?" He exited smoothly from the interstate.

"Oh, it's okay." She sighed. "The charm is wearing off some."

"It's been three years?"

"Almost four."

"Well, you're doing better than I thought you would. I thought you'd move back in a year or two."

"I've been thinking about it. I'd like to be closer to Mom and Dad."

Joel nodded his agreement. "I don't think you'd have trouble finding a job here. Indianapolis is a growing city."

Amy looked out at the familiar scenery flashing past. As a state auditor for Missouri, she'd traveled quite a bit. She had an apartment in Kansas City, but Cedar Valley, Indiana was home, and always would be.

She'd lived her whole life in the small community a few miles south of Indianapolis. After graduating from Indiana University near the top of her class, she'd moved to Kansas City. After nearly four years of city living, and real work in the real world, she was ready to concede that it wasn't all it was cracked up to be. Two weeks at home was just what she needed.

The first week would be devoted to Susan and the wedding. The second week she planned nothing more than rest and relaxation.

Dusk was settling over the ripening cornfields as Joel easily maneuvered the narrow country road. Amy rolled down her window and let the cool, fresh air tease her face and dark hair.

Joel looked over at her and smiled. Amy had always found pleasure in simple things. A cool summer breeze, a starlit summer night, the first snowfall of winter were all sure to please her.

He slowed the car and pulled into a gravel drive bordered by a variety of summer flowers and stopped in front of a two-car garage. Before Amy could gather her things, the car door was tugged open and Susan reached in to pull her out.

"There you are!" she cried. She wrapped Amy up in an exuberant hug.

Susan Hartman was a petite bundle of dynamite with an unruly cap of blond hair and blue eyes a shade darker than her brother's. Tiny bones and a creamy complexion only added to the illusion of fragility. Men instinctively wanted to protect her, until they spent ten minutes in her company and realized she neither wanted nor needed to be protected.

She drew back and looked at Amy. "I thought Joel forgot and left you stranded." The look she threw her brother was full of accusation.

"Me?" Joel protested, his remark punctuated by the firm thud of the car door closing. "You didn't even remember to tell her I was going to pick her up."

"I didn't?" Susan looked at Amy.

"Nope. But it's all right. You're entitled to forget a few things."

"Just so long as you remember to say 'I do.' "

Brad Drake, Susan's fiancé, came up behind her. The top of her head barely came to his shoulder. A serious leg injury had sidelined his pro football career, but he could still lift her with only one hand. His hair and eyes were as dark as hers were light and he possessed a rock-steady disposition just the opposite of her emotional nature. But he was every bit as crazy about her as she was about him.

He offered Amy an apologetic smile. "Sorry," he said sincerely. "Things are a little hectic."

"Hectic?" Joel shot his future brother-in-law a disbelieving look. "Princess Di's wedding preparations couldn't have been more complicated."

"Oh, that's real nice!" Susan retorted. "Do you have any idea of what I've had to keep track of these last few weeks?"

"Nope." He pushed the hatchback closed with a sharp snap. "I just know what I've had to keep track of."

She threw her hands up in exasperation. "I ask your help with a few little things and you get all bent out of shape."

"Come on, you two," Amy said soothingly. She had always been the peacemaker, and no siblings ever bickered better than Joel and Susan. But right now she was too tired for diplomacy.

"I need some coffee, and I need to put my feet up."

Brad took the hint, and Susan's hand. "C'mon, Susie," he said, tugging her toward the house. "Let's finish up those thank-you notes for the shower gifts. I'm sure Amy wants to see her folks."

"Come over in a little while?" Susan asked. She was staying with her mother until the wedding.

"Sure," Amy agreed. "Give me about a half hour." She turned to find Joel already cutting across the wide swathe of lawn that divided the two properties. Her mother was waiting at the back door of the renovated farmhouse.

Amy followed the faint path between the houses. It had been much more pronounced when she and Susan were kids. Now, after years of only occasional use, the grass was thick and green, and the path was barely noticeable.

"You look a little frayed around the edges," Brenda Michaels said.

Amy climbed the steps of the porch and smiled at her mother. Once again she hoped she would inherit whatever it was that kept her mother looking ten years younger than her forty-eight years. Her hair was still a rich auburn with only a few strands of gray. She wore it short and brushed back from her face in an easy style. Her eyes were sometimes green, sometimes gray, but always sparkling. When they exchanged a hug, Amy caught the scent of perfume she had come to associate with her mother. For as long as she could remember it had been the same.

"Frayed pretty well describes me," Amy said, drawing away. "You look calm, cool and collected as usual."

Brenda's eyes lit with amusement. "School's out," she said simply.

Amy laughed as she stepped into the large country kitchen. Her mother had been teaching elementary school for over twenty years. Like most teachers, she lived for summer vacation.

"We heard the commotion," Brenda said as the door closed. "I hope you can keep Joel and Susan in line."

Amy shook her head. "I thought I was the maid of honor, not the referee."

Brenda chuckled. "In this case, I think the roles are interchangeable."

"Don't I know it."

Amy cut through the dining room and stepped into the family room at the back of the house to greet her father. Neil Michaels looked up from his paper and removed his reading glasses. His dark eyes brightened at the sight of his daughter. Amy reached for his hand, reminded again of how much love she felt when her father looked at her. His hair was graying and thinning, but he was still the most handsome man in the world to her.

He rose, a little stiffly, drew her close and dropped a kiss on her cheek.

"Hi, Dad. Sorry I'm late."

"Not your fault. Joel should've—"

Amy interrupted. "That's him in the hallway."

"Well, tell him they'd better keep it down next door or I'll call the sheriff and all his dumb deputies."

She laughed. "Idle threats, Daddy, and you know it."

"Yeah, but I still enjoy making them."

It felt so good to be home. She was smiling as she left the room and continued down the hallway to find Joel. She turned to enter her room, and came to a jarring halt as she walked into the solid wall of his chest. She stumbled and nearly fell backward.

Joel reached out and caught her shoulders, holding her steady. "Are you all right?" he asked, looking at her closely.

She tried to answer, but found it hard to breathe, much less speak.

"Come sit down." He led her to the bed, and she gratefully dropped down to sit on the edge.

The mattress shifted as he sat beside her and draped an arm lightly across her shoulders.

"Take slow, deep breaths," he instructed, his voice pitched low.

She did as she was told and within seconds felt the tightness in her chest begin to ease. But she became acutely aware of Joel sitting close beside her. He seemed to radiate warmth and a masculine scent seeping into her senses caused a skittering awareness along her nerve endings. She lifted her head slowly and met his blue-eyed gaze.

Her lips parted on a quick, surprised breath. She wanted nothing more from life at that moment than to feel his mouth on hers.

Joel pushed to his feet and quickly put a healthy distance between them. He took a moment to gather his scattered wits. He had almost tasted the tempting sweetness of her mouth, had wanted to feel her body pressed close to his own. Nothing in the world could have prepared him for this surprise. Before turning to look at her, he drew in a deep breath.

"Are you okay?" To his credit, his voice was steady.

"Yes, thanks." She stood slowly, and her gaze darted around the room.

Finally, she turned her wary eyes to him and he saw the fading shadow of surprise still displayed there. Whatever had happened, she'd felt it, too.

"Thanks for the ride from the airport." Her voice sounded weak to her own ears. "Tell Susan I'll be over in a little while."

He nodded. "See you later." He left the room without a backward glance.

Amy stood frozen to the spot and listened absently as he spoke to her father. She waited, wanting to be certain Joel was gone before she ventured from the safety of her room. A shudder raced through her when she realized how close she'd come to making a complete fool of herself. Joel must be trying not to laugh. After all these years, little Amy Michaels had a crush on him? How cute.

Amy lay on her old twin bed, darkness surrounding her, and felt the soft summer breeze whisper across her skin.

She looked out her window into a velvet darkness alive with stars and the glow of a half-moon. As a young girl, she had spent countless summer nights just like this, thinking, and dreaming, and wondering who her true love would be.

Joel. She whispered his name. She could not get him out of her mind. How odd, to know him all her life and, within the span of a few hours, find herself wondering if she'd ever looked at him before.

What did she really know about him? His favorite color

was red. He liked fast cars, Colts football, and Indiana University basketball. He could be quick-tempered if pushed too far or your strongest ally when needed. He was one hundred percent committed to his family and the business he had started three years ago.

Amy looked out into the soft night and again pictured him at the airport. She'd been attracted to him—pure and simple. She'd suddenly seen him as a man, not a friend or big brother. And she'd caught another glimpse of that man in her bedroom. She'd wanted to kiss him! She could feel her cheeks redden with embarrassment. What had she been thinking of?

She was thinking of bright blue eyes, sandy brown hair, and a firm mouth just inches from her own. She was thinking of form-fitting blue jeans and a tee shirt covering solid muscle. She was thinking of Joel Hartman in a way she never had before.

She pushed the light summer blanket to the foot of the bed and gave up on sleep.

Shopping was not going well. Amy wanted something special for her best friend. She'd already purchased a wedding gift for the couple, but she wanted something personal for Susan.

She stepped out of another of the gift shops at the Valley Mall and glanced down at her watch. It confirmed what her growling stomach had been telling her for the last twenty minutes. It was lunchtime and she was starved.

She was headed for the food court when the sound of her name being called caught her attention. Turning to look over her shoulder, she stopped and stared.

"Oh, my gosh!" she cried as the dark haired man approached her. "I can't believe it's you!"

Mark James stopped in front of her, a pleased grin splitting his handsome face. "And I can't believe it's you." He wrapped his arms around her in a great bearhug. "How long has it been?"

She enjoyed the familiar strength of those arms a moment longer before stepping back. "About nine years, I guess." She studied him, realizing he had changed little over the years. He was wearing dark dress pants and a tailored blue shirt with the sleeves rolled up to his elbows. She could remember only a handful of times that she'd seen him in anything other than his favorite sweats or jeans. "You look wonderful."

"You do too, sweetheart." The endearment came easily. And for an instant they were both transported back to a time when love had been fresh and new and uncomplicated.

"So what are you doing here?" he asked. "Last I heard you were living in Kansas City."

"I still am. I'm here for Susan's wedding. You remember Susan Hartman, don't you?"

"Of course. You two were a matched set."

Amy laughed. "That's us."

"I saw her engagement announcement in the paper a while back. Is the wedding this weekend?"

Amy nodded. "Saturday afternoon. So what are you doing out shopping at this time of day?"

"I snuck out of the office. I'm on a mission. Tomorrow is my fiancée's birthday, and I have to find something fantastic for her."

"You're getting married?" Amy felt a flicker of emotion left over from dreams long ago put away.

"In September. Her name is Julie Morris."

"Congratulations. I'm happy for you."

Mark's dark eyes studied her. "What about you?"

She held up her ringless left hand. "I'm still foot-loose and fancy-free. And I've just about exhausted the eligible male market in Kansas City."

"Well, move back here."

"As a matter of fact, I might."

"Really?" His interest sharpened a notch. "Have you checked out the job market in Indy?"

She shook her head. "Not yet. But I'm going to."

Mark looked down at his watch, then back at her. "Have you had lunch yet?"

"No, and I'm starving!"

He laughed and dropped a friendly arm over her shoulders. "Come on. Let's go get something to eat. We can discuss your job qualifications while we eat."

"An offer a smart girl would never refuse."

The food court offered something for the health food nut and the junk food junkie, with plenty of variety in between. Amy chose a thick hamburger with all the trimmings minus the onions, an order of fries, and a chocolate shake.

Mark looked at her tray and at his meager ham sandwich and diet cola. Ruefully, he shook his head. "I swear, Amy, I never did understand how you could eat like that and still stay thin."

"Heredity."

"I guess it must be." He took a drink of his cola. "Tell me about your job."

"It's pretty simple. I'm an auditor for the state of Missouri. I go around to different companies and check their records to be sure that they're doing everything legally and within the set limits."

"A lot of detail work?"

"Are you kidding?" She rolled her eyes. "It's like being a detective. I usually have to go back and reconstruct everything to see exactly what steps were taken when." She shrugged. "It's not a job for just anyone."

"Do you enjoy it?"

She nibbled on a french fry thoughtfully. "I enjoy the challenge of the job. I like problem solving and organizing."

Mark nodded his understanding. "Have you heard of Miller Laboratories?"

She laughed shortly. "Sure. It's the biggest company in

Indianapolis. Everybody sent their résumés there when they graduated from college."

"So did I. I'm the personnel manager there."

Her brows shot up. "Are you really? I'm surprised my mother didn't tell me. She keeps me up-to-date on local gossip."

"Your mother has probably refrained from telling you anything about me since I very nearly corrupted you," he said.

"No way," she scoffed. "I corrupted you."

He grinned. "It was a mutual corruption."

"You bet it was."

He gazed at her a long moment. "I've got a proposition for you."

"Shame on you," she scolded, her eyes teasing. "You're practically a married man."

"This is a legitimate proposition," he explained. "There's a job opening at Miller Labs. Perfect for someone with your skills."

She stopped eating and looked at him wide-eyed. "Are you kidding?"

He shook his head.

"Tell me what I need to do to apply."

"I'll set up an interview. Let me check my calendar. I think next Wednesday is open. How's that for you?"

"I'll be there."

He dug a business card out of his wallet and handed it to her. "Call me Monday. We'll set up the time."

"Thanks!"

"Aren't you even going to ask me what kind of job it is?"

"Nope. You wouldn't have mentioned it if you didn't think I was qualified. We'll talk about it Wednesday."

"Okay." He stood up. "I've got to get a move on. Somewhere in this massive complex is the perfect gift for Julie, and I've got to find it before five o'clock."

Amy laughed. "Good luck."

"Thanks. See you next week."

"You bet you will," she assured him. She watched as he left the food court. He still moved like the athlete he'd been in high school, and when he'd hugged her, she'd felt the firm muscle beneath the dress shirt. The boy she'd known had turned into a very handsome man. A wry smile curved her mouth as she stood to leave. To think she'd let him get away nine years ago.

Two

Amy was kept so busy that Friday's arrival came as a surprise. She'd spent the week helping Susan stay calm. The bride-to-be was a basket case. Even though Amy was certain that every detail was in order, Susan was equally sure that a calamity waited around the next corner.

Tonight's wedding rehearsal and dinner were under control and on schedule, but Susan had phoned three times in the last hour to report that Joel was going to be a little late. This, to Susan, was a major problem. Amy offered all the comforting words she could and then hung up.

If Susan didn't leave her alone, she was going to be late, too.

Her mother's reflection joined her own in the mirror. "Can I help?" she offered.

Amy sighed. "Every time I get my hair just right, Susan calls, and I have to start over. She's really flying. Even I'm beginning to feel edgy."

Her mother smiled and began to work the pins into Amy's thick hair. "You've been her rock all these years. You can't let her down now."

Amy waved her hand in easy dismissal. "Oh, I won't. But this will be my last official duty as the rock. Brad's taking over my role tomorrow."

"Well, he seems to be quite capable of keeping up with Susan."

Amy rolled her eyes. "The man is crazy in love. He was

dazzled by Susan's blond hair and big blue eyes. Hasn't had a coherent thought since."

"Love is grand," Brenda murmured as she pulled tendrils of hair down from the chignon. After a moment she stepped back to inspect her handiwork. "You look lovely," she said simply.

Amy turned to look in the full length mirror. The sleeveless navy blue silk dress was simply cut, with a jewel neckline to show off the teardrop sapphire necklace given to her by her parents for her college graduation. The waist was cinched with a navy belt and the hem flared out gently just above her knees. Sheer hose adorned shapely legs and navy and white spectator pumps added two inches to her height.

"What a dish!" her father spoke from the doorway. He gave a low wolf-whistle.

"Oh, Daddy," she groaned, even as a smile curved her mouth. He grinned, his fatherly pride showing in his eyes. "Who's the lucky guy tonight?"

"Joel. He's driving me to the rehearsal and dinner." She looked down at her watch. "He's late."

Her father shrugged. "Must be a good reason. The boy's always been reliable."

Amy smiled. "The boy" was thirty-two years old, but she decided not to mention this fact to her father. "You remember that I'm going to spend the night with Susan, don't you?"

Both nodded just as the phone rang.

Sighing, Amy crossed the room and picked up the receiver. "Susan, honey, you've got to relax. Joel isn't here yet, but I'm sure he's on his way."

There was a pause before, "Hi. I *am* on my way."

"Oh. Sorry. I thought it was Susan again. She's really keyed up, Joel. I don't think I've ever seen her like this."

His low chuckle seemed to travel right through the phone to the pit of her stomach. "Just hang in there, sweetheart. It'll be over soon."

"I know. But *I'm* starting to get nervous."

"Oh, no!" Mock horror laced his words. "I can't have both of you falling apart at the same time."

"Can we take turns falling apart?"

His husky laughter drifted along the line again, and she found herself enjoying it thoroughly—again. A peculiar reaction, she decided, to something she'd heard a million times before.

"No. Listen—I'll be there in about fifteen minutes. Be ready."

"I'm ready now," she assured him. "See you."

Amy was waiting when Joel pulled into the driveway precisely twelve minutes later. As he got out of the car, he seemed to stop in his tracks. She couldn't see his eyes behind his sunglasses, but she saw the purely male smile curve his mouth. Her pulse raced.

She'd thought he looked fantastic in blue jeans. He was nothing short of devastating dressed in a tailored charcoal-gray suit. His crisp white shirt was sharply offset by a red silk tie. She wondered how she would react to him tomorrow when he would be wearing a tuxedo.

"You look sensational." His voice was pitched low and sent delicious shivers dancing along her spine.

"So do you," she said softly, her voice slightly unsteady.

Joel took her elbow and escorted her around the front of the car.

"Don't forget that's my daughter I'm trusting you with, young man," Neil called from the porch. He was leaning against the porch railing watching as if Amy was out on her first date.

Joel laughed and shook his head. "Why do I feel like I've stepped back in time about fifteen years?"

"Because I want you to feel like that," Neil teased. "It's a father's job."

"I'll take good care of her," Joel assured him as he

climbed into the sports car. He waved as he backed out of the drive.

"Is your pediatrician friend still out of town?" Amy asked, after they'd driven away.

"She'll be back tomorrow for the wedding."

Amy wondered what the woman would be like. If she was a doctor and could afford to drive this kind of car, then she was probably very sophisticated. Very unlike herself.

Amy mentally shook herself. Why did she feel so intimidated by a woman she had never met? And why did it matter anyway? Unconsciously, she straightened and crossed her legs.

The movement was not lost on Joel. His gaze drifted briefly to her legs before he focused back on the road. Amy was barely three feet away and her perfume had begun to wrap itself around him. He could almost see himself pulling the pins from her carefully styled hair and letting it fall freely to her shoulders. He imagined its silkiness in his hands, and—

Shocked to realize where his thoughts were leading, he quickly jerked himself back to reality. The sooner they got to the church, the better. He pressed on the gas pedal. The car shot forward and hummed smoothly along the narrow country road.

As expected, they were the last to arrive. The rehearsal went smoothly despite the good-natured teasing and wise-cracks. Everyone recognized the release of nervous tension for what it was. Come tomorrow it would be a totally different story and they all knew it.

Shortly after eleven they headed home. Joel's mother wanted a ride in the racy sports car, so Amy rode with Brad and Susan. In no time they arrived at Susan's house.

Amy immediately went upstairs and changed into a cool tank top and shorts. She was thankful they would be able to dress at the air-conditioned church tomorrow.

When she came back downstairs, she stopped in the

kitchen for one of Anne's fantastic homemade brownies before heading out to the front porch swing. Brad and Susan were loving each other up beside his car.

"It's bad luck for the groom to see the bride before the wedding," she called to the couple.

"That only applies on the wedding day, silly," Susan returned, her voice soft and dreamy.

"Well, I hate to break it to you, but in five minutes it will be your wedding day."

"Oh, my gosh!" Susan immediately backed out of Brad's embrace. "You've got to leave! Now!"

Amy could hear his frustrated sigh. "Thanks, Amy."

"You're welcome, Brad," she returned sweetly. She watched as he backed out of the driveway and then drove out of sight. Turning, she walked over and settled on the swing, setting an easy rhythm.

Susan came up the steps and leaned against one of the pillars. "I can't believe tomorrow I'll be Mrs. Bradley Drake. How did I get so lucky, Amy?"

"Beats me," Amy returned promptly. "If you've got a recipe for catching great guys like Brad, please share it with me."

"Oh, all you have to do is be yourself."

"It's not working for me so far," Amy said dryly.

"Don't worry, it will." A yawn punctuated her sentence. "I'm going to go change and then I'll be back out."

She disappeared inside just as Joel pulled into the driveway. The headlights caught Amy in their glow as he pulled around to the back of the house.

"What a ride!" Anne exclaimed as she and Joel came onto the porch. "I may have to get me one of those."

"And give me something else to worry about," Joel remarked.

"Of course, dear." A softly rounded, petite woman, Anne had to reach up a long way to pat his cheek. "We'll call it parent's revenge. It'll be my way of paying you back for all the gray hairs I've collected over the years."

"I was a model child," he said smugly.

"Sure you were." Sweet sarcasm dripped from her voice as she looked up at him with blue eyes that both of her children had inherited. Like her daughter Susan, she appeared small and fragile. And like her daughter, she was not. She possessed an inner strength that had been tested and could only be admired.

She was smiling as she turned toward the door. "I think I'll turn in. 'Night, kids."

Joel chuckled as she disappeared inside. "I'm going to miss my air-conditioning tonight," he said, as he shrugged out of his suit jacket and began to unknot his tie.

"Are you staying here?" Amy asked.

"Yeah. Susan's request." He draped his jacket and tie over the railing. "You staying, too?"

She nodded. "Susan's request."

His smile told her he understood. "Can I join you?"

"Sure." She scooted over to make room for him on the swing. He sat beside her and studied her a moment. "You let your hair down. I liked it up."

"Thank you. I wear it like that sometimes. For a change."

Slowly, he reached out and touched a soft curl. It was hard to tell who was more surprised by the action. They looked at one another steadily, their eyes mirroring each other's wariness. Gently, his hand glided through the silky strands, just touching her shoulders.

"You've always had beautiful hair," he said, his voice barely audible. A slight smile curved his mouth. "Except for the time Susan cut it for you."

Amy laughed at the memory, breaking the fragile thread of intimacy he'd created. "Oh, was that ever a mess!"

"How old were you guys?"

She thought a moment. "Probably about ten." She shook

her head. "The hairstyle we picked out of one of your mother's magazines was really cute."

"And short," he inserted.

"Yeah, very short. But Susan and I had no doubts that she could duplicate the style."

"That was your first mistake."

She looked over at him, her eyes shining with laughter. "Yup. I never trusted her with scissors again."

His laughter joined hers and floated on the night air. Amy was totally at ease and unprepared for the feel of his fingers on her cheek. Her gaze flew up to his and locked there. His finger softly traced along her jawline before stopping below her chin to tilt her face upward.

"Why hadn't I noticed," he said reflectively, "that you'd turned into a beautiful woman?"

Amy saw a light in his eyes that she'd never seen before. It seemed to send a surge of electricity along her nerve endings, creating a clash of sensations she'd never felt before. It was both exciting and frightening, and she didn't want it to ever end.

"Okay, I've got an idea!" Susan burst from the house, and it took Amy a moment to focus her eyes and mind again. She was only vaguely aware of Joel rising and walking to the far end of the porch.

"There's a full moon. Let's go for a walk," Susan suggested, excitement tingeing her voice.

Joel turned to frown at his sister. "What for?"

"Because I'm wound up tight and a long way from sleep," she answered honestly. "And besides, tomorrow I start a whole new chapter in my life." She shrugged helplessly. "I don't know, Joel. For a few hours I just want to go back. Like when we were kids."

He gazed at her and felt all the exasperation drain away. Susan stood there in cutoff jeans, a baggy tee shirt, and dirty tennis shoes looking very much like a kid. Tomorrow she took on the responsibilities of marriage. If she wanted to spend an hour or two meandering down a country road in the moonlight, who was he to deny her?

He sighed and laughed. "Why not?" He looked at Amy. "Want to come?" He saw the answer sparkling in her eyes.

"Yes! Hurry up and change."

He just shook his head as he walked into the house. "You two are priceless."

A full moon hung suspended in the sky, its glow casting obscure shadows as fireflies tirelessly danced over the cornfields, filling the night with eerie golden lights. A vast network of stars cast a mysterious canopy over the three figures walking down the middle of the lonely country road.

They walked in easy silence for at least an hour, each drinking in the beauty of the night and cherishing the memories that tied them together. A distant, welcoming light shone out from the porch to guide them home again, as it had shone when they were children. Whatever the future held, the past they had shared would bind their lives forever.

Amy felt tears sting her eyes as she watched Joel escort the stunning bride down the red-carpeted aisle. Her gaze shifted to Brad, and she was touched by the obvious love that shone in his eyes.

Susan was the essence of romance in a satin gown with a sweetheart neckline and full sleeves. A braided pearl necklace encircled her throat and her face was framed in heirloom lace. She had never looked more beautiful, or more fragile. Amy's heart went out to her.

Amy had always dreamed of a wedding like this. She wanted the yards of satin and silk, the abundance of flowers, the flowing music. But more than anything else, she wanted a man to look at her the way Brad looked at Susan as she came down the aisle.

When Susan and Joel reached the altar, he turned to her and gently lifted her veil. He paused, then bent to kiss her cheek.

She drew back and looked up at him with love-filled eyes. A radiant smiled curved her lips as she lifted a hand to rest against his cheek. "Thank you," she whispered and only those close by could hear. "You've done Daddy proud."

He caught her hand in his own and brushed a kiss against her fingertips. "Just be happy, sweetheart." His gaze lifted and met Brad's for a moment before he released Susan's hand and stepped back.

Amy felt two tears slide down her cheeks and didn't bother to try to hide them. Charles would have been proud indeed, and his spirit was a very real part of the ceremony.

Joel stood next to his mother as Susan and Brad joined hands. Amy avoided his eyes, afraid she'd turn into a heap of useless mush if she looked at him now.

The wedding went smoothly. There was no fainting bride, no stuttering groom, and no lost rings. Amy wondered what had happened to the nervous wreck who had driven her around the bend this past week. Susan was transformed, tranquil, and utterly dazzling.

"You look wonderful."

A slow smile curved her lips. "Thank you, Daddy."

Neil Michaels returned the smile. "Just stating the obvious."

Amy looked past his shoulder at the elaborately decorated banquet room. Couples crowded the dance floor as the catered meal was cleared away. She caught a glimpse of Joel. As she'd expected, he looked fantastic in the black tux and creamy shirt. He was dancing with Debra. Amy had met her earlier and found her to be very pleasant and unfairly gorgeous. As she watched, Joel laughed at something Debra said, and bent to kiss her cheek.

Amy looked away. For one fleeting moment she held the image in her mind of Joel bending to kiss *her* . . .

"The reception is going well."

She snapped her attention back to her father and pushed away the unsettling fantasy. "Everyone seems to be enjoying themselves."

Neil looked around the room. "Except your mother. Where is she?"

"Try the kitchen. She and Anne are probably telling the caterers how to handle the leftover food."

"You're probably right. I'll go see if I can find her and claim a dance."

The following hour passed in a happy blur of cake-cutting, garter-tossing, and an undignified squabble over the bride's bouquet. It was just after nine when Susan and Brad drove away, but the party didn't end. By ten o'clock, Amy was sure she was going to drop from sheer exhaustion.

She leaned wearily in the open doorway leading out onto the patio and watched the dwindling group on the dance floor. A hand came to rest on her shoulder, and she looked up into smiling blue eyes.

"You look tired," Joel said softly.

"Exhausted. How do we get these people to go home?"

"Turn off the lights."

"Wonderful idea. Where's the switch?"

He chuckled. "Not yet. The last dance's for me."

"What about Debra?"

"She left. She's on call tonight."

Amy tried not to look too pleased. "She seems very nice."

"She is nice."

The band was playing a romantic ballad as Joel took Amy's hand and led her out onto the deserted patio softly lit by paper lanterns. Music drifted through the open French doors, and she settled into the comfort of his arms. She didn't think about following his lead. It seemed natural to move with him. She put her head on his shoulder.

"Tired?"

She nodded.

"What? No moonlit stroll tonight?"

Amy laughed softly. "I don't think so."

"You can spend all next week resting. You've earned it."

"I have a job interview next week."

"In Indianapolis?"

Amy nodded.

"I ran into an old friend at the mall on Tuesday and we had lunch. He's the personnel director for Miller Laboratories."

"Miller pays well."

"Mm-hm. I might even be able to ask my favorite real estate agent to find me a house."

"Is that right?" A slow smile curved his mouth. "I could always use the business."

Her eyes lit with mischief. "How do you know I was talking about you?"

He shrugged lightly. "I thought I was your favorite everything."

She laughed again and shook her head. "It must be wonderful to be so self-assured. Does anything trip you up?"

"Sure. But you'll use it against me if I tell you."

She looked up at him thoughtfully, a long moment. He returned the gaze steadily. "Tell me."

"Careful, Amy. You might end up with more than you bargained for."

She shook her head. "I'm not afraid of you, Joel."

"Maybe you should be."

There was something in his eyes that she had never seen before. Something a little wild, just barely restrained. She wanted him more than ever.

"I'd trust you with my life," she whispered. Her pulse quickened as unmistakable desire flared in his eyes. The band was still playing in the background, but they were no longer dancing. A silky thread of electric tension vibrated in the air between them.

Amy felt a jolt of pure pleasure as his hand spanned her bare back, urging her closer. Gradually, she felt the hard lines of his body press against the softer curves of her own. As his head lowered toward her, her eyes closed and her lips opened to the soft pressure of his mouth. He drew back and she waited, perched on the edge of some mysterious precipice. When he bent again and covered her mouth fully with his own, she tumbled headfirst over the edge.

She clutched the solid muscle of his shoulders beneath the formal jacket and held on as intense and unfamiliar sensations swept through her. She remembered her earlier fantasy. Her imagination hadn't come close to the powerful erotic reality of this moment. It was a dark and thrilling ride she found herself on. And one she never wanted to end.

Slowly, she felt him drawing away. She wanted to pull him back, but didn't. She dropped her hands and opened her eyes. When she looked into his, she was fascinated by the turmoil she saw there. He may have been calling the shots, but he'd been as deeply affected as she had. She was sure of it.

"Mr. Hartman?"

Joel struggled to respond to the sound of his name.

He turned away and stepped inside to answer the question being asked of him, and spoke to the last of the guests as they left. When he finally returned to the patio, Amy was nowhere in sight.

He stood for a minute and let his mind go back over the kiss they'd shared. Had he really experienced the sweet sensation that seemed to have momentarily claimed his mind and weakened his knees? Or had a simple kiss shared with the girl next door somehow gotten completely blown out of proportion?

Three

Amy turned toward the early morning sunlight and let it warm her face. The porch swing moved silently to the rhythm she set.

She took a sip of steaming coffee and let her gaze drift to the house next door. Joel had spent the night at his mother's again. She'd heard him come in shortly after she'd gotten home the night before. She'd waited for him, actually. Sat in the darkness of her room, heart pounding, waiting for him to come home.

She sighed and set the cup aside. Her mind and her heart had been waging a fierce battle since Joel had kissed her. Logic reminded her that it had only been Joel, the boy next door. But her heart told her they'd stepped into uncharted territory last night. The rules were new, and the risks were greater.

The sound of a car door slamming caught her attention, and she looked up to see Joel turning away from his blue sedan and starting toward her house. He crossed the yard, and climbed the steps of her porch. He hesitated before he spoke.

"You're up early," he said quietly.

"So are you."

He nodded. "I couldn't sleep."

"Me either."

His intense gaze didn't leave her face. "You know we're going to have to talk about it."

"I know."

He smiled slightly, satisfied with her brief answers. "Let's go fly a kite."

Her eyes widened. "What?"

"I've got a really neat kite. Fully loaded. String de-tangler, anti-tree radar, the works. Never fails."

Amy laughed. He never ceased to amaze her. "Give me a minute to get my shoes and sunglasses."

The bright paper kite soared high above the earth, seeming to touch the fluffy white clouds. Amy leaned back on her elbows and watched. Joel released more string, and the gentle breeze carried it higher still.

He turned to look at her over his shoulder and grinned. "See. I told you it never failed."

"Did I argue?"

"No, you know better."

Her laughter drifted on the wind. "One thing I've learned over the years is never to disagree with you when it comes to kites."

"Smart girl."

She sat up and rested her chin on her knees as she scanned the open landscape.

In the distance sunlight glinted off the upper story windows of the old Radley place. An idea began to form in her mind. She turned to Joel. "Who owns the Radley place now?"

He shook his head. "I'm not sure. Last I heard, the heirs were fighting over the property. There are close to two hundred acres total."

"That house could be beautiful."

"Needs a lot of fixing-up."

"I was in it once when I was little. I still remember the winding staircase in the entry hall. The sunshine was streaming in. I remember there was a white baby grand piano sitting in one corner."

Joel looked over at her. "Made quite an impression on you, huh?"

She nodded. "Do you think it will ever come on the market?"

"I think the land will be sold to developers."

"How sad." She sighed and lay back on the blanket, looking up at a deep blue sky filled with puffy clouds.

He moved over to join her.

"You're going to get the string tangled in that tree if you aren't careful," Amy warned.

"Nah. I haven't lost a kite to a tree since I was ten."

"It sure is up there. It's going to take you a half hour to bring it down."

He snapped the string and let the kite go. It soared and danced. Amy sat back up.

"Joel!"

"It's fun to set them free."

"You haven't changed."

He put his arm around her, and his free hand played with the yielding softness of her hair. When his mouth found hers, she immediately responded, granting him an answer both exciting and frightening in its intensity.

He groaned softly and deepened the kiss as her arms slid around his waist and her hands began to move tentatively over his back. He stretched out beside her, his hands making a slow, thorough journey over her shoulders and her sides. Fingertips brushed her breasts sending electric currents of pleasure coursing through her. Easily, he maneuvered past the hem on her cotton shirt and Amy shifted, relishing his caress on her heated skin. Her hands drifted to his hips, holding him as she fit her body to his. A tremor of pure desire raced through him, leaving him weak and needy. She matched him kiss for kiss, touch for touch, with no hesitation.

Amy hadn't lied when she'd told him that she'd trust him with her life. She thought she'd been in love before. But nothing had ever come close to the all-encompassing desire that consumed her now. She'd never wanted a man this way before, and how it had happened was a mystery. The fact that it had happened was a certainty.

Her fiery response to his kiss pulled Joel deeper into a thrilling whirlpool. He wanted to drown in her. Never had he imagined this kind of emotion. Not from Amy. Never from his Amy.

Distinct, sharp images of her exploded inside his head. At six, clinging to the top of the maple tree calling for him to help her get down. At twelve, asking him to be the first to sign the cast on her broken arm. At fifteen, coming to him for advice on boys. At seventeen, being the only one to see him cry after his father's death. Yesterday, telling him that she'd trust him with her life.

So much life between them.

Dear God. What was he doing?

Amy was completely unprepared when Joel bolted upright and turned his back to her. Confused, she murmured his name and reached up to touch his shoulder. He pulled away roughly and her hand dropped back to her side. She blinked against sudden tears, the sharp sting of rejection washing over her.

Joel lifted a hand and slashed it through his hair. He was trembling as raw emotion vibrated through his body. Never had he experienced desire like this. He'd always prided himself on his self-control. But he'd lost all semblance of that control just now, wanting nothing more than to make love to her in the sunlight.

He moved to put some distance between them. Amy stood and began to shake the blanket and fold it.

She walked over to stand facing him. The fact that he couldn't, or wouldn't, look at her hurt more than she ever would have guessed. "I'm sorry you find me too repulsive to look at."

His eyes instantly went to her. She could clearly read the depths of uncertainty there.

"You know that's not true," he said.

"Okay. Then what is it?"

He turned his attention to something, anything in the distance. He didn't know how to answer her or how to explain what had happened to himself, much less her.

After a moment he let out a deep breath, then pinned her with intense blue eyes. "You don't know how close I came to . . ." His voice faltered. Damn it! He felt like a fumbling teenager.

"To making love to me?" she supplied.

"Yeah." He bit the word out. "Damn it, Amy. It's not right."

"Because it's me." Her voice was hollow with pain, and the sound pierced his heart.

"Yes, because it's you." He gripped her shoulders tightly. "My God, Amy, you mean the world to me. I can't think of you that way."

"You can't, Joel, or you think you shouldn't?" she asked sharply. "I'm not your sister. I'm a grown-up woman, Joel, and ten minutes ago all I wanted was you." She pushed his hands away. "Now all I want is to go home."

She whirled away and started toward the car. He watched her go, completely dumbfounded. A door had opened that revealed a new side to a woman he thought he knew everything about. As stunned as he was at this moment, he was afraid that the temptation to find out more would prove to be stronger than his will to resist.

Amy relived the Sunday morning episode at least a thousand times. And each time she came to the same conclusion: she wouldn't have done anything differently. But Joel's reaction had hurt. She knew instinctively that his response had been as overwhelming as her own. She'd felt the desire coiled tightly inside him. It *had* been there, even if he wanted to deny it.

"I'm ready to go." Her mother's voice interrupted her reverie.

Amy patted her purse. "I've got my credit cards right here. I'm ready to shop till I drop."

Brenda laughed as she turned to lock the door. "Then let's get going. We've only got two days until your job interview."

They arrived at the Valley Mall shortly after the doors opened.

The first three boutiques had price tags that made Amy flinch. They hit the racks at four more before she found what she wanted in a price range she could afford. The summer suit had a plaid jacket in pastel colors of pink, mint, and cream and a slim, solid pink skirt. She found a blouse on sale, and a perfect pair of no-pinch dress pumps.

They left the mall at one o'clock and headed for a nearby diner.

Amy slid herself and the shopping bags into a corner booth. They were greeted by a smiling waitress who handed them each a menu.

Amy frowned and read aloud. "Fries, home fries, or mashed potatoes. Yikes! I've put on five pounds this week as it is."

"Really? *I* didn't force-feed you."

Amy lifted her head and grinned at her mother. "It was the silent threats that did it."

"Sure." Brenda looked at the entrance and a smile lit her features. "Look who's here."

Amy turned just in time to see Joel and Debra enter the dining area. Before she could say anything, her mother was waving them over and inviting them to share their table.

Amy managed a tiny smile, and made a silent vow never to eat lunch with her mother again.

"Oh, Amy, you can't believe how happy I am."

Amy smiled. Susan's contentment came right through the telephone line. "Yes, I can."

"Brad and I would like for you to come to dinner before you have to go back to Kansas City on Sunday. How's tomorrow night?"

"Are you cooking?" Amy asked suspiciously. Susan's lack of talent in the kitchen was just cause for Amy's cautious query.

"Good grief, no!" Susan sounded appalled at the suggestion. Much to her mother's dismay, Susan had never really caught on to the fine art of preparing edible meals. She considered it a stroke of luck that she'd fallen in love with a man who loved to cook. Her mother considered it a miracle straight from heaven.

"Brad cooks," Susan explained. "I mean really cooks. No frozen stuff."

"Are you sure he doesn't have a brother?" Amy asked.

"Nope. You met his entire family at the wedding. Only sisters."

"Darn. Oh, well. What time is dinner?"

"Six okay?"

"Fine with me. Mom and Dad are leaving in the morning for an overnight trip to Chicago, so I'll be on my own tomorrow evening."

"Wonderful. We'll spend the evening together. Wait till you see the pictures we took in Jamaica. You won't believe there's a place that beautiful on earth."

"It sounds fun, Susan."

"Good. We'll see you then."

* * *

Susan threw her arms around Amy's neck and nearly strangled her in her exuberance. "I'm so glad to see you!"

Amy laughed as she returned the hug. When she disengaged herself, she said, "Okay, let me look at you."

Susan lifted her arms wide and turned in a circle. "Well? Do I pass inspection?"

The tropical sun had tinged Susan's skin a delicate golden hue, seeming to deepen the blue of her eyes and lighten her blond hair. But Amy suspected the glow that radiated from her friend had nothing to do with the sun. Marriage agreed with Susan.

"You look wonderful." Amy's gaze went past Susan to where Brad leaned in the arched kitchen doorway. "I can see you're treating her right."

"Does this mean I've passed all the stages of inspection?" He came to hug Amy. "First Anne, then Joel, now you. That's everybody, isn't it?"

"Hey, when you married her, you got the rest of us in the bargain." She reached up to pinch his cheek. "What a deal!"

"Well, personally I think I got the best end of the deal." Joel stepped out of the kitchen, a can of soda in his hand. "I don't have to worry about her anymore."

Susan lifted her chin defensively. "When have I ever caused you any trouble?"

"Let's see. Should I start with your birth?"

"Come on, you two," Brad intervened. "No bickering. Amy's here." He turned to Amy. "Can I get you something to drink?"

"A glass of wine," Susan answered for her. "I'll get it." She caught Brad's hand and tugged him into the kitchen with her.

Joel looked across the room to Amy and whispered conspiratorially, "Susan isn't cooking."

"I know. That's why I agreed to come."

He nodded knowingly. "Me, too." Susan's lack of talent in the kitchen was legendary.

They took a moment to look around the newly decorated living room. The two-bedroom bungalow was located in the heart of a historic neighborhood on the east side of Indianapolis. Susan had been immediately charmed by the little house despite its rundown condition.

Amy could see that a fresh coat of ivory paint on the walls and ceilings and new beige carpeting on the floor had been just what the small room needed to give it an open feeling. Susan had cleverly arranged a brightly patterned sofa and two chairs along with a mahogany coffee table and end tables. The room felt wonderfully comfortable and homey.

Joel settled on the sofa and propped his feet up on the coffee table, looking very much at home. "Have a seat," he invited. When she chose a chair across from him, he fixed her with a curious stare. "Afraid, Amy?"

"Cautious," she admitted.

"Smart girl." He took a drink of his cola and watched her over the top of the can. He felt an edginess he couldn't explain, and it had everything to do with her. It was very disturbing, in more ways than one.

"How did your job interview go?" he asked, deciding a neutral subject would be safest for them both.

"Really well, I think. The job would be a little different from what I've been doing, but that's okay. I think I'll like it."

"What job is this?" Susan asked as she handed Amy the goblet of wine. She turned to sit on the sofa beside Joel.

"Auditor for Miller Laboratories."

Brad whistled from the doorway. "People line up to try to get their foot in that door. How'd you luck out?"

"A friend told me about an opening." She shrugged. "He's the personnel manager there and arranged an interview for me."

"Who is he?" Susan asked, her curiosity stirred. "Anyone I know?"

Amy smiled mischievously. "Mark James."

Susan's mouth opened, but nothing came out. Her eyes widened. "You've got to be kidding!" she breathed. "You ran into Mark James and didn't tell me about it?"

"Well, you were busy getting married," Amy pointed out.

"Oh." Susan seemed to consider a moment. "I guess that's a good reason."

"Who is Mark James?" Joel asked, looking from his sister to Amy.

"Yeah," Brad chimed in, pinning his wife of one week with curious eyes. "Who is this guy?"

"Don't look at me like that!" Susan protested, batting innocent blue eyes at her husband. "I hardly remember the guy."

"Yeah, right," Joel snorted. "You're practically drooling, Susan."

"I am not! Mark was Amy's pulse pumper, not mine."

Joel nearly choked on his drink. "Pulse pumper?" he asked, incredulous. "That's how you referred to guys you were interested in?"

"No." Susan's tone was indignant. "That's how we referred to Mark James."

"So who is this guy?" Brad asked. He waved a hand at Susan when she began to answer. "Not you. You're a happily married woman, remember? You're not supposed to be thinking about other men. Let Amy answer."

Susan smiled up at her husband and said demurely, "Yes, dear."

"Oh, brother!" Joel looked askance at his sister's sudden docility.

"Come on, Amy, tell us about the pulse pumper," Brad insisted.

"Mark was a year ahead of us. Undoubtedly the best-looking guy in school. He wasn't particularly tall, but he was very—ah—athletic. But better than all that, he was nice and intelligent. The all-American nice guy."

"And Amy had a crush on him," Joel inserted smugly.

"No," Susan said slowly. "Amy nearly married him."

Disbelief flashed across Joel's face. "When?"

"The summer before our senior year in high school."

"What?" Joel sounded stunned. "How did I miss all this?"

"We didn't want you to know," Susan said matter-of-factly. She turned back to Amy. "So, what's he like now?"

"About the same. Still handsome and still—athletic. It was good seeing him again."

"Wouldn't it be great if you got back together? Maybe he's just been waiting for you, Amy."

"I don't . . ."

"Wait a minute." Joel leaned forward, the teasing gone from his voice. "I want the whole story. How did you almost marry this guy?"

Amy considered him a moment, curious about his demanding tone. She wondered if it was Joel the big brother who was interested or Joel the man. "Mark and I dated toward the end of my junior year and were together the summer before he went off to college. We thought we were in love. We almost eloped."

Joel stared at her as if she'd just sprouted wings, then turned his attention to his sister. "And you knew all about this?"

"Sure. Amy and I have no secrets."

He turned back to Amy, an odd expression on his face. "Why didn't you do it?"

She regarded him a long moment, her eyes eloquent. "Because your dad died. Everything changed for me that day."

Silence filled the room, and Amy found herself having to look away from the emotion in Joel's eyes. The sudden buzz of the oven timer pierced the air, and both Brad and Susan moved to respond.

Joel pushed to his feet and crossed to Amy's chair. He reached out a hand, and she took it without hesitation. Rising, she looked up at him. His fingers came up to brush her cheek with a feather light caress.

"He loved you, too." His voice was husky, unsteady.

"I know."

"Come on, you two," Susan called from the kitchen. "It's ready."

Amy couldn't break away from his intense study. She wondered what he saw, wondered if he could see the truth of the feelings she made no effort to hide.

"Who are you, Amy?" he whispered.

Smiling softly, she captured his hand with her own. Slowly, she brought it to her lips and placed a kiss on his palm, her eyes never leaving his.

Joel felt his legs weaken. What kind of magic did she possess that allowed her to nearly bring him to his knees with a single kiss?

She turned to go to the dining room, but he stood transfixed for a moment longer. How was it possible to know so little about someone he'd known forever?

Four

Amy leaned forward to slip on her shoes. The grandfather clock in the hallway had just struck one. "I've got to get home," she announced. "It's way past my bedtime."

"Well, when you move back here we can get together more often," Susan said.

"I have to have a job first." She stood. "Where did I put my purse?"

Joel reached for the dark bag sitting next to his chair and pushed to his feet. "Here." He held it out to her. "I'm driving you home."

"Don't be silly," she scoffed, searching for her keys.

A jingling from his vicinity caught her attention. She looked to see her keys dangling from his fingertip. "I'm driving," he said again. "You've had three glasses of wine. I counted."

Her eyes widened with insult. "I'm not drunk."

"I didn't say you were. I'd just feel better driving you home. It's late. The roads are slick from the rain. Humor me."

She shrugged carelessly and turned toward the door. "Suit yourself. Just seems like a waste of time to me, but it's your time."

Joel followed her to the door, and a chorus of goodnights were exchanged before the two found themselves alone in his car.

"How will I get Mom's car tomorrow?" she asked, as he backed out of the driveway.

"Don't worry about it."

A light mist was falling as they started the twenty minute drive to Amy's house. Joel turned on the radio and soft music blended with the hypnotic rhythm of the windshield wipers. Lightning flashed and skittered across the sky, briefly brightening the scenery.

Amy knew she should thank him for driving her home. She didn't like being out so late by herself, and she didn't like going home to the secluded and empty house. She just wished he would have offered instead of ordered. But her mind began to wander, and the soft lull of the music combined with the soporific effects of the wine soon had her eyes closing.

Joel glanced over at her and smiled. Her face was turned toward him, her breathing deep and even. She was out like a light, and he was glad he'd insisted on driving her home. Dark lashes rested on her cheeks, and her hair was a dark cloud framing her face. In sleep she looked soft and young . . . and innocent.

He turned his attention back to the wet road and let his mind drift back over the evening. It amazed him that the little girl next door had grown up, and he hadn't even started to notice until she'd come home this time. It terrified him that now, when he'd recognized the change, that she could so easily destroy his self-control. She threatened to steal away his usual levelheadedness. He doubted that she was even aware of the power she wielded.

When he pulled into her driveway and drew to a stop in front of the garage, she didn't stir. He studied her profile as the interior of the car was illuminated by a flash of erratic lightning. The desire to kiss her came at him from somewhere deep inside. A misty image formed in his mind and intensified until the desire became a restless need. Her lips were

soft and full, slightly parted in sleep. The thought of coaxing
a response from those lips had him leaning toward her.

He shouldn't touch her.

Gently, he traced the fullness of her bottom lip with his
thumb. She murmured something and moved her head
slightly. He trailed a fingertip down her cheek, then continued downward along her neck to trace along the collar of
her silk shirt. She turned her face toward him and slowly her
eyes opened. He watched, expecting her to awaken and pull
away. But as a sleepy awareness came into her eyes, she
didn't move. She waited, as if she knew instinctively that
this moment was inevitable.

Trust-filled amber eyes seemed to search his very soul.

He should stop while there was still time.

The gold buttons of her shirt were freed with barely an
effort on his part. Like a whisper, his hand slid beneath the
fabric, caressing the sensitive skin. His slow hand moved
upward and stopped at the thin, lacy bra that cupped her
smooth, warm breasts.

Amy's eyes closed for a moment as pure pleasure seeped
through her system to the very core of her being. Her breath
caught and she waited, suspended in time, captured by the
magic he worked. Then, gently, reluctantly, she eased away
from him and opened the car door.

As silent as shadows, hands entwined, they entered the
house and slipped down the hallway to her room. No words
were spoken. None were needed.

She turned without hesitation and looked up into the eyes
of a man she was sure she would love forever. He reached
to gather her close. *This is Joel,* her mind whispered. His
familiar scent surrounded her, his strong hands spanned her
back as he bent to kiss her. His mouth claimed hers at last.
Passion that had been smoldering just below the surface
flared to life, consuming them in an instant. Lingering
doubts faded into nothing as pure emotion ruled freely.

Amy's fingers dug into the solid muscle of his shoulders

as his lips began to journey downward along her neck and shoulder. With impatient hands he pulled her silk shirt out of the waistband of her slacks and tossed it aside. Her skin heated despite the damp night air. Joel's fingers drifted lazily downward as his lips teased the upper curve of her breast. She released the side button of her slacks allowing them to slide down her legs to the floor. He touched her then, his hands skimming lightly over her hips, along her spine, across her stomach. She responded to his teasing by wrapping her arms tightly around his neck and arching her body into his. With a moan he had no knowledge of making, his mouth found hers again for a deep, melting kiss.

Amy wasn't sure if her legs gave out or if Joel chose that instant to lift her off the floor and carry her to the bed. The cotton sheets felt cool against her skin. Lightning flickered outside the window, casting a half light into the room. She watched as he removed his own clothes, scattering them carelessly about the room. His body was taut, with finely defined muscles, and she reached for him eagerly as he came down beside her on the narrow bed.

There was no rush to their first lovemaking. Each touch, each taste, revealed something new, something exciting and unexpected and special.

They explored and teased until passion exploded, consuming them with desire, thrusting them into a world brimming with dazzling sensual wonders. They gave and took in equal measure until finally, together, they gave each other the ultimate of pleasures.

Amy dozed, her head nestled against Joel's shoulder. Her breath sighed warmly over his skin, and her hand rested possessively on his chest. Joel toyed absently with her dark hair, letting his fingers glide in and out of the silky curls. He could still taste her on his lips. Their combined scents lingered in the heavy air.

He stared into the night and wondered if his mind had somehow tricked his body into believing that what had happened had been as perfect as it seemed. In thirty-two years he had never come close to experiencing the sexual intensity she provoked in him. His mind had shut down to everything but the pleasure that seemed to flow from her body to his.

His hand drifted down to rest on the curve of her hip. She felt slight and fragile beneath his touch now, but there had been nothing weak about the way she had loved him. Her response had been strong and sure.

A sudden slash of lightning drenched the room, followed immediately by a long, vibrating rumble of thunder. Amy stirred, stretched, and enjoyed the delicious friction of her skin rubbing against his. She tilted her head back and opened lazy eyes. He was watching her with renewed passion, and she felt his fingers tighten restlessly in her hair. A purely feminine smile curved her lips as she realized and contemplated her newfound power. Slowly, her fingers traced lightly down his body. She heard his breath catch and felt his body tense. Watching him, her excitement grew, and she let her hand continue to wander.

"I like you like this," she said, her voice a husky murmur. "I've never known you to be anything but strong. It's nice to know you have one weakness."

"You just like being able to bring a man to his knees."

"No." Amy raised up on an elbow and looked down into his face. She shook her head. "Not just any man, Joel. Only you."

For a split second the sensual daze surrounding him parted, and he could see everything revealed in the amber eyes he knew so well. She kept no secrets. Her trust and her love, freely given, were there for his taking. She didn't even have to say the words.

Fear, strong and terrifying, clenched in his stomach. He needed to put a stop to this, for her sake and his own. But her hands were like satin on his skin, moving again, teasing and tantalizing. And her mouth was on his body, leaving a trail of moist kisses that turned his soul inside out.

Electricity from the ensuing storm crackled in the air, echoing the sultry tension in the room. And Joel made the only decision he could.

His hands dove into her hair, holding her head still as his mouth drank deeply from hers. Her fingers dug into his back, and he rolled until she was beneath him, her body matched perfectly to his. Driven by a need and desperation he didn't fully understand, he focused only on her pleasure and everything else just slipped away. The chains of doubt, the ache of knowing he was going to hurt her, faded into nothing. He was going to take her somewhere she'd never dreamed existed. A place where her mind, body, and soul would meet and join for a few precious moments with his.

Damn tomorrow and the sorrow it promised to bring. For this brief space of time he was going to show her heaven.

The first hesitant light of the new day filtered into the room as Joel quietly pulled on his jeans. His mother rose early in the summer and liked to enjoy her first cup of coffee on the patio. It wouldn't do for her to step outside and see his car parked in Amy's driveway at five in the morning, especially since her parents were away.

He looked around the room, making sure he had everything. His gaze went to Amy. Even as the pastel sheet concealed her body, it hinted at the curves beneath. She was curled on her side, as if he still lay in the narrow bed beside her. Unruly dark curls fanned out over the light pillowcase. His palms tingled as he remembered the silky strands sliding through his hands. Sleep softened her delicate features and emphasized her fragile beauty.

He couldn't seem to pull his gaze away from her. A hundred different emotions fought within his heart. He'd broken every rule, shattered every illusion of what he believed to be true. Together they'd crossed an invisible line. There was no way to ever go back.

The passion of the night seemed unreal now, almost dreamlike. In the dim morning light he felt alone and strangely bereft. He wondered if they'd traded something very precious for a few hours of fleeting pleasure.

He wanted to touch her, hold her, assure himself that nothing had changed. Drawn by the same need that had brought him here, he reached toward her. And then he stopped. Everything had changed. The innocence of their relationship was gone forever.

For the first time in his adult life, Joel found himself literally paralyzed by fear. He didn't know what to say or what to do. If Amy opened her eyes now, he wasn't sure if he would fall to his knees and beg her forgiveness, or crawl back into the bed and make love to her again as the morning sun played over her skin.

He raked a hand through hair already mussed and nearly laughed out loud. Even through the thick fog that seemed to have settled inside his brain he knew he was close to coming apart.

He had to get out of there.

When he slipped out of the house moments later, the birds were just beginning their morning chorus. No one saw him drive away.

Neil Michaels peered at his daughter over the top of his newspaper. She swayed gently in the swing, the movement unconscious. A magazine lay open in her lap. He was sure, however, that she had not turned a page in the last half hour. She was a million miles away, lost in thought. She'd been distracted like this since he and Brenda had returned home from Chicago earlier in the afternoon. He knew something was up, but Amy gave no clue as to what it might be.

He put his paper aside. "Are you feeling okay, honey?"

Her eyes seemed to focus on him from a distance far away. "What?"

"Are you feeling okay?"

"Oh. Sure." Her smile was faint. "Why do you ask?"

"You're awfully quiet. I thought something might be wrong."

Amy felt nerves quiver in her stomach. "I was at Susan's pretty late last night. I'm just tired, I guess."

Neil looked down at his watch. It was just after seven. "Maybe we ought to go get your Mom's car. It's getting pretty late."

Amy's emotions were raw. She'd waited the whole day for Joel to return the car, or at least call. But with each passing minute, his silence stretched tighter between them, twisting around her heart.

She stood. "I'll call Susan—maybe he's there." She started inside, but stopped when she heard the sound of an approaching car. Joel pulled into the driveway and parked in front of the garage.

Amy went down the steps to meet him, sure the light had come on in her world. He climbed out of the car, and she was surprised to see him dressed in a dark blue suit.

"Hi." His gaze rested on her briefly before shifting to her father. "How was your trip, Neil?"

"About the same as usual. I'm always glad I don't have to live in Chicago."

"Yeah, I know what you mean."

The purr of another car had them all turning to watch as Joel's car came to a stop behind Brenda's. The door opened and Debra slid out, dressed in a sequined black dress that emphasized her figure to perfection.

"Good heavens, Joel," she said, sounding exasperated. "You drive these country roads like A. J. Foyt."

"Sorry." His boyish grin obviously won her over as he walked toward her. "I forgot you hadn't been here before."

She smiled up at him and took his hand. "Okay," she conceded softly. "This time."

Debra spoke to Neil, and Amy found herself making all the proper responses when Debra spoke to her. Amazing. She could make small talk as her heart broke piece by piece. Joel didn't look at her, didn't even seem to notice that she was there. In some detached corner of her mind she began to doubt that last night had been real. Perhaps it had all been a dream. Perhaps she'd wanted it so badly that her mind had simply manufactured it in graphic, intimate detail.

"We'd better get going, Joel, or we're going to be late," Debra said. "It was nice seeing you again, Mr. Michaels."

"You, too."

Joel escorted Debra to the passenger side and opened the door for her. When he came back around the front of the car his attention was fixed on the car keys in his hand. Amy waited, needing him to look at her. When he reached to open his car door, she spoke his name softly.

She saw his hesitation, watched his shoulders tense. For one moment, she thought he was going to ignore her completely. Then, slowly he turned, and she looked into shuttered blue eyes. She wanted to touch him, to see if the walls he'd built around himself could be brought down. If last night had been real, she was sure she could reach him. But she couldn't touch him, wouldn't touch him now, when he so obviously wanted to forget their night together had ever existed.

"Thank you." Her voice was level, pride keeping the pain from revealing itself. "For bringing me home last night and for taking care of the car. I appreciate it."

Joel saw everything she didn't say displayed clearly in her eloquent eyes. The urge to go to her slammed into him, but he stood rooted to the spot. Protecting, soothing, being there for Amy was an integral part of his nature. It was inconceivable that he was the cause of the pain he saw so clearly in her eyes. But he knew it was true.

As he stood there undecided, he watched the light in her amber eyes flicker and die. A dull emptiness quietly banked the last ray of hope. She had always been sunshine and laughter, her smile enough to brighten the darkest day. Looking at her now he wondered if she would ever smile again. How could he have caused her such pain? How could he leave her like this?

He wanted to plead for her forgiveness. Despite the exquisite pleasure they'd shared, he still couldn't see past the little girl in pigtails and cutoff jeans. He couldn't reconcile that Amy with the woman he'd made passionate love to last night.

His chest grew tight with profound regret. He'd never intended to hurt her. There were no words to be said, none he could have said right then. Forcing himself to move, he merely nodded and turned to slide behind the wheel of the car.

As he drove away his heart and mind fought a fierce battle. His mind tried to convince him that anything as intensely fulfilling as what they'd shared could never last. His heart called him every kind of fool. What they had shared could only come once in a lifetime. He had just walked away from it.

The job offer from Miller Laboratories came two weeks after Amy returned to Kansas City. Mark James left the message on her answering machine. If she decided to accept it, she could give her notice at work tomorrow.

She sat at her kitchen table, sunshine streaming through the glass balcony doors. It was nearly noon and she hadn't yet bothered to shower. She was dressed in a sloppy pair of shorts and a tee shirt that had seen one too many washings.

Listlessly, she sighed and looked down into her steaming coffee, wondering again if she should take the job. It was a wonderful opportunity, no doubt about it, but it meant

moving back to Indianapolis. That meant being close to
Joel. It was unbelievable how painful that thought was.

A month ago she would never have believed that the
thought of Joel Hartman could hurt so. In all the years of
growing up he'd never hurt her. Bullied her, maybe, annoyed
her, yes. But he had never intentionally hurt her. Never. She
looked up at the wall calendar. Never, until twenty days ago.

God, how she hated keeping track. It was stupid and
weak, but she couldn't help it. She was so helplessly in
love and so unhappy about it that she'd made herself ill.
She'd felt physically ill when Joel had driven away with
Debra that Saturday evening. The feeling had stayed with
her since coming back to Kansas City.

Nausea plagued her night and day, leaving her unable to
look at most foods, let alone eat them. She'd already lost
seven pounds. Her head ached, she wasn't sleeping well,
and she felt like crying ninety percent of the time. She was
miserable, plain and simple, and it was all Joel's fault. Or
maybe it was all hers. She wasn't sure anymore. All she
knew for sure was that she missed him desperately.

The phone rang, and she didn't even move from her chair.
The machine was on and she let it answer.

Susan's cheerful voice filled the room. "Hi, Amy. I was
wondering if you've heard yet about the Miller Labs job—"

Amy picked up the receiver. "Hi."

"Amy? What are you doing home on a Thursday morning?
Playing hooky?"

"Oh, something like that." She pushed a hand through
her tangled hair. "I got the job."

"Wonderful! When will you move back?"

"In about three weeks. I've got to give the great state of
Missouri two weeks' notice."

"Amy, it's going to be great having you home again.
Where do you want to live? Should I have Joel find something for you?"

"No." Amy answered sharply. "Don't bother Joel. I'm

not sure exactly where I want to live yet. Now you'd better get back to work before you get fired for goofing off on company time."

"Okay—but keep in touch."

"I promise."

"Hey—maybe this will get you and Mark back together."

Amy's eyes closed wearily. "Mark is engaged. He's getting married in September."

"Oh, shoot!" Susan sounded genuinely sorry. "That's too bad. I was hoping for a fairy tale ending."

"Not for my story." Amy's voice nearly broke.

There was a lengthy pause before Susan spoke again. "Are you sure you're okay, Amy? You don't sound quite like yourself."

The tears that sprang into Amy's eyes didn't really come as a surprise. All it took was a gentle note of concern in her best friend's voice to do her in. But Joel's betrayal wasn't something she could share with Susan. Not now. Not ever.

Swallowing hard, she managed to steady her voice. "I'm just really tired, that's all. I've been working late, and this job change has been on my mind. Don't worry about me."

"Well, you get some rest," Susan said hesitantly, as if she wasn't quite convinced by the words she heard.

"I'll be fine," Amy assured her. "Listen, I've got to run. I'll call you soon."

"Okay. Don't forget."

After goodbyes were exchanged, Amy replaced the receiver and felt hot tears spill over and trace down her cheeks. God, she was a mess.

Rubbing the heels of her hands roughly against her eyes, she turned and headed for the bathroom. Damn Joel anyway.

But one thought kept nagging at the back of her mind. If she couldn't get over him here, how did she ever hope to be able to live in the same city with him?

Five

Joel stared into space, the signed purchase agreement on his desk all but forgotten for the moment. Amy was coming home—for good. Susan had called a few minutes ago with the news.

Two distinct images seemed to be seared into his brain and free to haunt him at will. The first was of Amy the morning he'd left her curled up in bed, peaceful and sated following their exquisite lovemaking. Unaware of his churning thoughts and scrambled feelings, and unaware of the heartache that awaited her.

The second was of Amy as he'd gotten into the car with Debra that Saturday evening and driven away. He'd seen the disbelief and pain in her amber eyes. From that point on, guilt had become his constant and formidable companion. He'd broken Amy's heart and betrayed her trust.

Dropping his pen to the desktop, he leaned forward and rubbed his hands over his face. God, how could he have been so callous? He'd never before experienced anything as intense as he had with Amy that stormy night. And because it was her, he hadn't known how to handle it.

From the moment he'd stopped the car in her driveway and she'd opened her eyes, he hadn't thought about the consequences of what was about to happen. It seemed inconceivable to him now that he hadn't given a passing thought to the risk they were taking. The magnitude of his actions had multiplied until he was sure he would fold under the pressure.

Debra's call, reminding him of their date, had spurred him to action. He had to do something. At the very least, he had to get Amy's car back to her.

During the drive to her house that evening he'd agonized over what to say to her. When he'd stepped out of the car and encountered the sparkling warmth in her eyes, he'd lost all ability to think, much less speak. In the end, he'd said nothing, effectively shattering her on the spot.

Since the moment he'd driven away with Debra, thoughts of Amy filled his mind and haunted his sleep. Purposely, he tried to recall every phase of her life, from baby to little girl to teenager. He had watched her grow alongside Susan and had always assumed that he knew all there was to know about her.

Yet he hadn't known that she'd been in love at seventeen and willing to make a commitment based on that love. He hadn't known what a profound effect his father's death had had on her. And he hadn't known that she possessed the power to create a flame of yearning in him that would not die.

That was where all his logic broke down. In two short weeks, the innocent girl next door had turned into a passionate, loving woman who had unexpectedly turned his orderly world upside down. And she'd done it fully expecting him to recognize the special gift she was offering him. Amy had trusted him with her heart. Foolishly, he had refused to accept it.

He wondered how she was doing. He wondered if she despised him. She had every right to. But she'd told him once that she could never stay angry at him for long. He'd clung desperately to the hope that it was still true.

Twice he had mustered up the courage to phone her. Both times her machine had answered. He hadn't had the courage to leave a message. What he needed to say couldn't be said to a machine.

With a sigh of resignation he picked up his pen. She was

coming home, and he'd see her soon. He kept telling himself
it would be okay. This was his Amy. He'd explain his feelings to her and pray that she would try to understand. They'd
work this out and move past it. To what, he still wasn't
sure. He was sure, however, that he needed Amy back in
his life. The hole she'd left in his soul six weeks ago was
big enough to drive an eighteen wheeler through.

The scent of hamburgers sizzling on a charcoal fire
drifted in the late afternoon air. Neil Michaels was cele-
brating his fifty-fifth birthday with the traditional family
cookout. Amy sat in the porch swing and wished she had
the energy to join Susan and Brad in their game of bad-
minton. But the August humidity sapped every ounce of
strength she had.

Since returning home, her mother had been after her almost daily to see the doctor for a checkup. Amy had finally
relented and was going in tomorrow afternoon.

Brenda was more than a little concerned about the change
in her daughter. Something was very wrong, but Amy hadn't
sought her out to talk about it. On the one occasion that
Brenda had tried to ask some questions, Amy had quickly
cut her off.

Actually, everyone in both of the families had noticed
the change in Amy, except Joel. He hadn't seen her since
she'd moved back, but was expected this Sunday afternoon.

Amy didn't expect Joel to show up. He'd been avoiding
her since she had returned. She knew she had every right to
be angry with him. He'd taken something beautiful and re-
duced it to nothing more than an act of sexual release. In
doing so he was not only destroying something precious, but
he was destroying everything they'd ever been to each other.
The easy friendship would be gone forever. She wondered
if she grieved for the loss of that more than anything else.

"Hamburgers are ready, Amy. Come get one," Neil called from the grill.

Amy didn't want a hamburger any more than she wanted anything else on the heavily laden picnic table. But she took one anyway and walked over to the table.

"Where's Joel?" Susan asked as she slid in next to Amy. "He usually calls if he's going to be late."

"Probably with a client." Brad squeezed ketchup onto his hamburger bun. "He's been pretty busy lately."

"Yeah, maybe," Susan murmured uneasily.

Brad looked at his wife. "Yeah, maybe what? You don't sound convinced, little sister."

"Well, I'm not," she returned defensively. "Something's up with him."

"Could be Debra. Maybe she's popped the question."

At Brad's suggestion, Amy felt the few bites of food she'd eaten turn to stone in her stomach.

"No way." Susan shook her head and reached for the potato salad. "He's not even seeing Debra that much anymore."

Anne frowned. "I didn't know that."

"Too bad," Neil said as he sat down with his plate of food. "They make a really cute couple."

"Just like Ken and Barbie," Susan put in dryly. "Plastic and perfect."

"Good grief," Brad chided. "You're pleasant today."

"Well, I'm sorry, but I can't help it. Debra is nice enough, but she isn't what Joel needs."

Amy's mother came down the steps carrying another pitcher of iced tea. "Joel just called," she announced. "He'll be here in fifteen minutes."

Amy felt every nerve in her body react. How was she going to face him? He'd been so cold the last time she'd seen him. She knew she couldn't bear his indifference this time.

She carried her half-full plate to the trash can under a nearby tree. Dropping it into the bag, she could feel five sets of eyes on her back.

"You didn't eat very much." Her father made the comment lightly, but she heard his underlying concern.

She walked back to the table and picked up her glass of iced tea. "It's too hot to eat. I'm going to cool off next to the air conditioner for a while."

With that she walked away, leaving an uncomfortable silence behind her. The cool air felt wonderful against her flushed skin as she went to her bed to lie down. She closed her eyes and forced her mind to empty. Within minutes she was sound asleep.

She was still asleep forty-five minutes later. Susan stood for a moment in her doorway and hesitated.

Amy stirred. Her eyes opened and focused on Susan's face. Slowly, she pushed herself up into a sitting position. "Was I asleep long?"

"About an hour. Your dad is waiting to open his gifts and cut that cake. He's like a big kid."

A small smile drifted across Amy's features. "Yeah, I know."

Susan sat on the edge of the bed. She reached across and took Amy's hand. "Why won't you tell me what's wrong, Amy? I'm worried about you."

Amy let out an irritable sigh. "I feel like I'm under a magnifying glass all of a sudden. Why are all of you so certain something's wrong with me?"

"Because we know you. And we love you."

"Well, you're all about to smother me with love." She jerked her hand away and began to rub her forehead. "I'm just tired."

Susan sat thoughtfully for a moment before speaking. "I know you're not just tired, Amy. I know you're hurting, and I want to help. But I don't know how unless you tell me."

Amy felt tears threatening and knew if they started, there would be no stopping them. Susan's words tore at her already battered heart, but she couldn't tell her best friend what was troubling her. Joel had driven a wedge between her and Susan. She'd already lost Joel's friendship. She wouldn't risk losing Susan's.

She turned to her. "Give me some time, okay?" she said softly. "I need to work this one out for myself."

Hurt clouded Susan's blue eyes, but she smiled through it. "I just want you to know that I'm here any time you need me."

"Thanks." On impulse, Amy leaned over and hugged her friend. When she pulled away she pasted a smile on her face and stood. "We better get outside or Dad will have my hide."

Joel looked up when Amy came out of the house and stopped what he was saying in midsentence. The sight of her alarmed him. She looked frail. The red and white tee shirt and red knit shorts that hung on her body attested to lost weight. The emptiness radiating from her eyes tore at his heart. It was worse than he remembered, worse than he could have imagined.

"I'm sorry, Daddy." She bent and kissed Neil's cheek. "I fell asleep."

"That's okay, sweetie." He patted the bench. "Sit. Have some cake."

She sat beside him and joined in the fun. She sang a round of "Happy Birthday" and clapped as he blew out all fifty-five candles. She did her best to down a piece of cake and a bowl of ice cream and laughed along with the others when her father opened the gag gifts they'd bought for him.

To anyone looking on she appeared to be having a good time. But Joel knew things were far from okay with Amy. He also knew he was the cause.

With the setting sun came the sirenlike sound of the locusts. Amy sat on the porch swing with her mother and enjoyed the cooling breeze. Susan sat dozing in a chaise lounge, and Anne worked on her crossstitch. The three men had disappeared into Neil's workshop in the back of the garage.

It was a typical summer evening in the Midwest, laid back and peaceful.

"Well, if this isn't one lazy group," Neil teased as he and the two younger men approached the porch.

"Yeah, look at Susan over there sawing logs," Joel teased.

"I am not sawing logs," she said with dignity. "I am resting my eyes."

"Forgive me for not knowing the difference."

She stood and stretched. "Well, since everyone is here— Brad and I would like to make an announcement."

She walked over to her husband's side and slid her arm around his waist. She was nearly beaming when she turned to the expectant group and said, "We're going to have a baby."

There was a split second of stunned silence before everyone began to speak at once. Susan looked as if she'd stolen the sun from the sky. Happiness and contentment seemed to pour out of her as she attempted to answer everyone at once.

Amy had always felt that she'd never had much use for envy in her life. It seemed like a wasted emotion, one usually manufactured by the mind. But as she sat there watching Susan, she actually begrudged her friend the joy she was experiencing. And the knowledge of what was in her heart left her feeling ashamed and wretched.

Amy rose and went to Susan. She hugged her best friend close and then reached up to kiss Brad's cheek. "Congratulations. Your baby is going to have two wonderful parents."

Susan looked into Amy's eyes, not understanding the turmoil she saw there, but recognizing the sincerity of her words. With a trembling smile she wrapped her arms around her again.

Nearly twenty minutes later, Amy found herself alone on the porch. Susan and Brad had gone home, her parents were inside, and Joel had walked next door with his mother.

She stretched out in the chaise lounge and watched as the sunset bled various shades of red and pink into the sky. She closed her eyes.

Milestones in her life flashed across her mind. She'd grown up surrounded by love and protected from most of the world's injustices. Each day had faded into the next, and life required few sacrifices of her.

Charles's death had been her first real taste of life's unfairness. He'd left for work one morning and hadn't come back. A massive heart attack had claimed him and all life-saving measures had proved useless. He was gone almost instantly.

His death forced Amy to take a serious look at the life she was planning for herself. In the cold light of reality it didn't take her long to realize that eloping with Mark was wrong for both of them. Telling him had been one of the hardest things she'd ever had to do. They had parted, aware of what they had given each other and with no malice between them.

Life took funny little twists and turns, and all you could do was hang on for the ride. She was barely hanging on now. The unexpected, exciting path she'd started out on with Joel was turning into a lonely and desolate journey. Though she'd not yet found the courage to face it, she knew exactly what awaited her next.

"Amy?"

Her eyes flew open and her heart pounded rapidly in her chest.

"I'm sorry," Joel said quietly. "I thought you heard me come back."

He studied her, the blue eyes seeing past any pretense she might have offered. "Let's go for a walk." Noting her hesitation, he added gently, "Please. I think we better talk."

A tense silence hummed between them as they walked down the narrow country road toward the creek. The sun was gone, but the sky still glowed with muted light. When they reached the one-lane iron bridge, they stopped, and Joel bent to pick up a handful of pebbles to toss into the water.

"Talk to me. About that night," he said.

"Little late for that. Or should I be grateful for better late than never?"

He heard the bitterness in her voice and knew he deserved nothing less. He pitched a rock into the water. It landed with a thick plop.

"I left without waking you for two reasons. One, I didn't want Mom to get up and find my car in your driveway. Two, I didn't know what to say to you."

She thought about that a moment. "Oh, I see. You didn't know what to say, so you said nothing. You just pretended it had never happened."

"Try to understand," he began carefully. "I was terrified of what had happened. You've always been like a sister to me. And then suddenly you weren't. I didn't know how to handle it."

She met his gaze directly. In the dim light he searched for a spark of hope in her amber eyes. There was none.

"It was nothing but sex for you." She spoke with such cold certainty that it took him a moment to respond.

"No." Her accusation caused a ripple of shock to race through him. He lifted his hand to touch her cheek and was stunned when she jerked away. "Amy," he whispered, stricken. "What have I done to you?"

"You treated me like a one night stand. I trusted you with my heart, Joel. And the very next day you're out on the town with Debra, and you won't even talk to me. I was foolish enough to think that what we shared was special. But you were just playing the game. Guess you won."

"Amy, you mean the world to me. How can you think that I would intentionally hurt you like that?" He paused, trying to detect some softening in her features. "I'll take the blame for a lot of things, but I wasn't playing games."

"Then we won't play any games now." Pent-up emotion

swamped her and her voice broke. She struggled for control and finally won.

"I'm pregnant."

"What?" The word came out on a disbelieving breath. Out of nowhere an invisible fist planted itself in his stomach. He dropped his head and closed his eyes, searching desperately for something to stabilize his spinning world. In some detached corner of his mind he wondered why he was even surprised. All caution had been tossed to the wind that night. The thought of protecting her had not even so much as entered his mind.

"In case you're wondering, the baby is yours."

Her bitter words pierced his soul. He looked up into her shattered eyes.

"I don't doubt it, Amy." He wanted to hold her, help shoulder some of the burden she'd been carrying alone all these weeks. "I'm sorry."

Infinite sadness filled her eyes. "I know," she whispered.

"No," he said quickly. "I didn't mean I'm sorry about the baby. I'm sorry I let you down."

She stared at him impassively. "It doesn't matter now."

"It does," he insisted. God, he wanted to shake her, do anything to spark some emotion in her. He caught her arms, tightening his grip when she tried to pull free. "We can figure this out, Amy. Let's decide what our options are."

She looked at him blankly, then gave a short, disbelieving laugh. "Options, Joel? I have none. The only thing I can do is give birth to this child and love him. The only thing you can do is acknowledge that this baby is yours and love him, too. There are no other options. Sorry."

"We'll get married."

"Why?" she asked bluntly, amazed at his suggestion. "You don't love me."

"That's not true. I've always loved you."

"You're talking about the little girl next door, your sort-of little sister. That kind of love isn't going to work in a marriage, Joel."

"Dammit, Amy," he flared, unable to contain his mounting frustrations. "Will you at least try to understand?" He released her arms. "I've been trying like hell to work out what my feelings for you are. After we made love . . ." He hesitated, searching her eyes, willing her to believe him. "I have never felt anything that strong and perfect before. That's the honest truth, Amy." He stopped again, trying to see into her mind, into her soul. "Maybe it was love. Maybe it will be."

"And if it's not? What then?"

"I can't see into the future. All I know is that I want this baby to have my name. I want to take care of you."

"Fine. But let's not lie to ourselves. You're marrying me because you feel guilty, and you want this child to have your name. But you don't love me."

Her voice was as bleak as her eyes. Desperately, he wished there was some way he could make her believe that everything would work out. He was a long way from believing it himself right now.

"You're seeing the doctor tomorrow?" he asked.

"Yes. At four o'clock."

"May I go with you?"

She shrugged carelessly. "If you want."

"Don't close me out, Amy," he said quietly. "I want to be a part of this."

A faint, sad smile curved her lips. She turned and started back toward the house.

He watched her go. There was nothing more to say.

Six

Amy sighed as she studied her computer screen. She wasn't thinking clearly, and the numbers on the screen made no sense. She closed her eyes a moment and brought a hand up to rub her forehead. Lack of sleep and food had turned an early morning ache into a deep, steady thud.

Reaching out, she punched a button on the keyboard, clearing the screen. She caught the phone on the first ring and the receptionist informed her that Joel Hartman was on his way up to her office.

Amy replaced the receiver and tried to steady her jumpy nerves. She wished now that she hadn't agreed to let Joel go with her to the doctor today. His presence wasn't going to alter the outcome of her visit. If anything, his involvement was making her feel even more anxious.

A faint sound at her open door drew her attention. Expecting Joel, she was surprised to see Mark there.

"Oh, hi," she said, standing.

"Got your e-mail. Thought I'd stop in while I was up on this floor. What can I do for you?"

"Well, I'm having a problem with information I got from the accounting department, and I thought you might be able to help me with it." She saw Joel in the hallway. "Oh. Can we talk about it later?"

"Sure." Mark, sensing the presence behind him, turned. "Excuse me," he said, moving into Amy's office and out of the doorway.

"I don't want to interrupt anything. I can wait out here."

"No, come on in." He extended his hand. "I'm Mark James."

Joel returned the handshake. "Joel Hartman. Nice to meet you." *Amy's first love.* He felt the slow burn of jealousy, something he had never felt before. But then, Amy had brought out a lot of things in him that he'd never felt before. "Amy's told me about you."

Mark shot a surprised look at her. "Oh. Well, Amy and I go way back," he replied cautiously.

"Yeah. I guess you do."

Mark was smart enough to know it was time to leave. He smiled at Amy. "Call me. I'm free tomorrow morning."

She nodded her agreement and stood silently as he went out the door. She could feel Joel's eyes on her as she gathered up her purse and locked the desk.

"Are you doing okay?" he asked softly.

She straightened and met his gaze directly. "I'm sick and I'm scared. What do you think?"

He accepted the blow without flinching. "Don't make me the enemy, Amy. That's not fair to either of us."

She came around the desk and started toward the door. "Don't talk to me about fair," she said as she passed by.

He stood for a moment feeling helpless. She was a stranger. Everything he knew about her, everything they'd shared, meant nothing now.

Joel waved to his neighbor, Ken Hudson, as he got out of the car. Ken straightened from his task of weeding the flower bed and waved back.

"How's it going?" he called.

"Pretty good, I guess." Joel came around the back of the car as Amy emerged from the passenger side. He felt her stiffen when he reached for her elbow and let his hand drop away.

"Hey, Joel, don't forget about the Saturday cookout."

Joel was uncomfortably aware of Ken's curiosity as he escorted Amy up the sidewalk leading to the front door. "I'll be there," he called over his shoulder before disappearing into the house.

"You'd better be. Or they'll talk about you," Amy remarked, once they were inside. "Or maybe they're used to you parading women in and out of your house."

Joel took a deep breath and managed to hold on to his temper. Barely. Since they'd left the doctor's office thirty minutes ago, Amy had been doing her best to start a fight.

The wide entryway opened into a huge great-room with a high beamed ceiling and thick gray carpeting. A brick fireplace centered between two bookcases dominated one wall, and a wraparound sofa and two recliners were arranged in front of an entertainment system. It was a comfortable room and neat as a pin.

"Can I get you something to drink?" Joel offered.

"Some milk?" she answered sarcastically.

"Okay, that's enough." He caught her arm before she could turn away. "Tell me what's going on, Amy."

"I'm pregnant," she said bluntly, her voice suddenly dull. "The doctor didn't tell me anything I didn't already know. I've been so sick that I've lost eleven pounds, and he says that has to stop. I need to eat and take vitamins and relax. I hate the sight of food, I detest taking pills, and I'm so stressed out that I can't even sleep at night." She paused and took a shaky breath.

"Satisfied?"

Silently, he turned away and walked into the kitchen. He had to stay calm. Amy was beyond reason both physically and emotionally. He reached into the refrigerator and pulled out a cold soft drink. Leaning against the counter he popped the top and took a long swig.

They'd be married, of that he was sure. Telling their parents was going to hurt—all of them. Once they were past

that, Amy could relax. When they were married, he'd see
to it that she ate regularly and rested as much as needed.

He had no illusions, however, that their life together
would be bliss. She was scared, she was angry with him
for getting her pregnant, and she had been hurt. She considered any marriage between them a sham. Unfortunately,
she was probably right.

He became aware of the heavy silence in the house and
walked back into the great-room. He didn't see her, and an
uneasiness overtook him. He moved further into the room
and then saw her. She was curled up on the sofa, asleep.

Joel quietly crossed the room and crouched beside her.
Her cheeks were flushed and still damp from tears, but her
breathing was deep and even.

He longed to hold her in his arms and protect her from
all her fears. He wanted to press his hand against her belly
and connect with the miracle they had created there.

But he didn't touch her. He knew she needed rest. And
he also knew that she wouldn't welcome his touch.

He stood and lifted the afghan her mother had made him
from the back of the sofa. As he gently spread it over her,
she stirred and murmured something but didn't open her
eyes.

He gazed at her, reminded of the morning he'd left her
sleeping in her own bed. Remembering the passion they'd
shared sent a heat rising through his body. For a few short
hours they'd been perfectly attuned to one another. They'd
barely spoken, each aware of what the other needed. How
could he have turned his back on something so rare? How
was he able to take something so precious and treat it so
lightly?

He'd been scared, plain and simple. He'd glimpsed his
future that night and it was so totally different from anything he'd ever planned that he'd attempted to run just as
far and as fast as he could.

Now there was nowhere to run. His past and future had

come together, and there was nothing to do but make it work. It would take time and patience, he knew. If Amy still loved him, it would be deeply buried beneath her resentment and pain. He'd have to chip away at all the layers of heartache until he found that love, and then he'd claim it for his own. All he had to do in the meantime was figure out a way to hold on to her.

Amy awoke abruptly as something cold and wet pushed itself against her cheek. The large green eyes staring back at her merely blinked. She sat up just as Joel came into the room and looked down at the huge black cat rubbing gently against her side.

"Your cat nearly scared me to death," she said crossly, even as she reached out to scratch its ears. The satisfied purring could be heard across the room where Joel stood.

"Well, you've made a friend for life now," he informed her. "Her name is Muffins."

Amy looked up and smiled softly. "Muffins? What kind of name is that for a cat?"

Joel felt the reaction to that unguarded smile in the pit of his stomach. He was suddenly aware of how much he'd missed her. "Susan gave her to me," he answered, his voice low. "She named her Muffins."

"Oh." Amy stroked the thick fur as the cat curled up beside her. "Then I guess Muffins fits."

She looked up, and across the room their eyes locked and held. For an instant time stood still. She needed for him to hold her. He needed for her to reach for him. Neither made the first move, and the moment disappeared when she turned her attention back to the cat.

"How long did I sleep?"

"A little over an hour. I'm sorry the cat woke you."

"It's okay. I need to get back and pick up my car. I should get home."

"Why don't you eat first? I've grilled some chicken and fixed baked potatoes."

She shook her head. "No, thanks. I'm not hungry."

"You need to eat."

She looked at him, drawn by the note of concern in his voice.

"Please." He tried a different approach. "You've got to feed the baby."

His words had the impact of a physical blow. "Fine," she said shortly. "I'll be there in a minute. Where's your bathroom?"

He directed her down the hallway. She closed the door and leaned against it as hot tears traced down her cheeks. She brushed at them furiously and went to the sink to splash her face with cold water. When she met her reflection in the mirror, a stranger stared back.

"You're such a fool," she berated herself harshly. "He doesn't care about you. It's the baby he cares about. If you want to survive, you'd better remember that. He's never going to love you like you want. Never."

Oh, God, how she wanted out of this nightmare. How much more could she take? She'd lost so much already, and now she was losing Joel further to the life her body was nurturing deep inside. She despised him for this unnatural jealousy she felt toward her own child. She despised herself for still loving the man who caused her such pain.

Susan stared at Joel and then shifted wary eyes to Amy. "If this is a joke, it's not funny."

Amy began to restlessly pace the length of Susan's living room. "Do you see anyone laughing? This is no joke. Trust me."

Susan looked back at her brother. She saw the stark truth in his eyes and much more she didn't understand. Rarely was she left speechless. But she could think of absolutely nothing to say.

Joel sensed her dilemma and reached for her hand. "It's going to be okay," he assured her. "We're getting married a week from Saturday. Will you guys be our witnesses?"

"Yes," Brad answered immediately. "We'll do whatever you need."

"Thanks." He gave Susan's hand a quick squeeze before releasing it and wondered if the uncertainty he saw in her eyes was merely a reflection of his own.

"Have you told your parents?" Brad asked.

"They're next."

"Yeah." Amy gave a sharp laugh as she turned to face the three of them. "Joel thought we'd try our technique out on you and Susan first. Since Susan seems nearly comatose, I think we need to come up with something a little less shocking." Her eyes darted to Joel.

"What else can we say? There just isn't any way to tell them you're pregnant without shocking them."

"Sure there is." Amy gestured toward Susan. "Susan looked up at Brad with adoring eyes and said 'We're going to have a baby,' and they all loved it. Maybe we should try that."

She began to pace again. Brad stood and went to her. He caught her shoulders in his big hands and said gently, "Come on and sit down. It'll be okay. They'll understand."

"Understand what, Brad?" She looked up into his face, searching, as if he might have some magical answer for her. "For God's sake, I'm not some teenager who didn't think about the consequences. I'm twenty-six, and I knew the risks. I took them anyway, and for what? Joel didn't love me then and he certainly doesn't now. And any love I felt for him is stone dead." She stopped and took an unsteady breath.

"So how are they going to understand, Brad?" Amy continued. "I don't even understand."

She walked over and dropped down onto the sofa. Leaning back against the thick cushions she wearily closed her eyes. Susan motioned for the two men to leave the room. She got up from the chair and went over to sit beside Amy on the sofa.

"Hey," she said softly, reaching for her hand. "Let's talk. Okay?"

Amy didn't open her eyes, but her fingers clenched around Susan's as if she'd finally found a lifeline to cling to. "You're right," Susan continued, "I am shocked. That doesn't mean I'm unhappy about it. I can't think of anyone I'd rather Joel married than you."

"He doesn't love me, Susan," she said tonelessly.

"That's not true. He's loved you forever, but he may not know yet that he loves you the way a man loves a woman. Give him some time."

"Well, he's got about seven months left."

"Amy, don't be bitter, please. It's not good for you."

Amy opened her eyes and looked at her friend. "Me or the baby?" she challenged.

"You. I love you. I want you to be happy."

Tears welled up in the amber eyes. "I trusted him, Susan, with my heart and soul, and he just turned his back on me. He left while I was still asleep and acted like it had never happened. All I wanted was to love him forever."

Susan gathered her friend close and let her cry. She suspected that this was the first time Amy had talked to anyone about what had really hurt her. Susan felt torn in half. She loved her brother, but she understood Amy's sense of betrayal.

Amy reached for a tissue from the box on the end table. She looked at Susan with a trembling smile. "I've cried enough tears in the last two months to drown a rain forest."

"You're making up for all those years when you were the tough one and I blubbered my way through life."

"Remember the crying bucket your dad used to get out

of the basement when you'd start in? He'd come back with it and his galoshes on, and you'd always start laughing."

"Yeah, he had me figured out," Susan said. "Him standing there with that stupid yellow bucket and big boots on always made me smile. Just like Joel can."

Amy's smile faded, and she remembered how the years had been filled with more laughter than tears. Joel had always been able to brighten her mood, with a silly joke or antic, or just by being there when she needed him.

"You know, Amy, you're not alone in this. Joel knew those risks, too. And he's older and supposedly wiser." She paused and chose her next words carefully. "You and Joel are the two most levelheaded people I know. I can't help but believe that there must have been something pretty special for you both to take such a serious risk."

The emotion that entered Amy's eyes was nearly breathtaking in its intensity and purity. "It was perfect," she whispered, remembering. "And despite all that's happened, I don't regret it."

Susan had never heard such conviction from Amy before. What could Joel have been thinking? Was he strong enough to win back the love he'd pushed away?

"Do you love him?"

Amy nodded. "I can't change that. I've tried."

Susan reached for Amy's hand.

"I feel so stupid, Susan." She drew in a ragged breath. "I'm supposed to be a responsible adult. How am I supposed to explain this to our parents?"

"Just tell them how it is and go on from there."

A sad smile touched Amy's mouth. "That easy, huh?"

Susan stood and pulled Amy to her feet. "I didn't say it was going to be easy." She laughed softly. "Come on. Let's see if we can get Brad to whip up some dinner."

Amy followed Susan into the kitchen. For the first time in weeks the thought of food didn't completely turn her stomach. Confession must truly be good for the soul.

* * *

The three parents each took the news with varying degrees of disbelief. Neil couldn't put a single word to the deluge of feelings that washed over him. Slowly, he rose and walked from the room.

The disappointment on her father's face nearly broke Amy's heart.

Her mother cleared her throat and said softly, "Well. At least now I know what's going on."

"What are your plans?" Anne directed the question to her son.

"We're getting married a week from Saturday."

"How do you plan to live together when you can't even look at one another now?"

Joel returned his mother's gaze squarely. "We'll work it out, Mom. Just give us time."

Amy's silence had not gone unnoticed by the two women. Anne turned to her. "How do you feel, Amy? Are you willing to work it out?"

Amy hesitated, twisting the ring on her finger, feeling trapped and unsure. "What other choice do I have?"

"Entering into a marriage based on anything other than love is a hard way to live," Brenda warned gently. "Marrying Joel just to give this baby a name may not be the best thing for any of you."

Amy stared at her mother. She couldn't believe what she was hearing. "Are you suggesting that I have this child out of wedlock?"

The phrase sounded so old-fashioned that Brenda nearly smiled. "No. But you're not exactly thinking clearly right now. Maybe you should wait a while."

"No," Joel said firmly. "We're getting married. I'll take care of Amy. We'll work out the rest as we go." He got up. "I'm going to speak to Neil."

At the sound of the back door closing behind him, Brenda turned her gaze to Anne. "He sounds pretty determined."

Anne nodded. "Yes, he does."

"Good." The two mothers exchanged a knowing look.

Amy had the distinct impression that Joel had just passed some kind of maternal test, but she wasn't sure what.

The two women turned their attention back to her. "Now," her mother said briskly, "what are we going to do about you?"

"What did the doctor tell you?" Anne asked.

"That I need to relax, and I can't lose any more weight."

Anne grinned. "Well, we can see that you don't lose any more weight."

"And you might as well relax because we still love you, no matter what," Brenda added.

"What about Daddy?"

Anne smiled reassuringly. "Don't worry about him, honey. Joel will take care of it."

Amy looked from one loving face to the other and felt as if a huge weight had been lifted from her shoulders. Reaching out a hand to each of them, they shared a three-fold hug.

Joel found Neil in the workshop busily sanding a piece of shaped wood. He didn't look up or pause.

A long moment passed, and Joel watched as Neil stopped sanding and rubbed the smooth wood with his hand. "I thought you'd find your way out here," he said without raising his head.

"I thought we needed to talk."

Neil nodded and reached again for the sandpaper. He began work on the other side of the wood piece. "Let me tell you something, Joel," he said quietly. "Brenda and I never expected to have a child. Her doctors told her she would never be able to conceive. I knew that when I married her.

And even though I had always wanted children, I was willing to give that dream up because I loved her so much."

He paused and tested the smoothness of the wood with his finger. "Amy was a miracle, plain and simple. When we discovered Brenda was pregnant, it was the happiest day of our lives."

Neil picked up a cloth to wipe up the dust.

"You're a fine young man, Joel. I know your dad would have been proud of you. I can't think of anyone I'd rather see Amy marry. But there's something bothering me."

His eyes met Joel's directly for the first time. "When I looked at you two in there earlier I didn't see love in your eyes or hers. I saw fear. That's no way to begin a marriage."

"I'll take care of Amy, Neil. You don't have to worry about that."

"I'm not worried about you taking care of her. I'm worried about you loving her."

Joel struggled to find words to explain something he didn't fully understand himself. "Amy's hurt and angry right now. She has a right to be."

Neil studied the younger man for a long moment. "I just want her to be happy again."

Joel nodded. "Me, too." He pushed to his feet and walked to the door. He reached for the handle, then stopped and looked over his shoulder. Neil had gone back to sanding.

"I promise I'll take good care of your miracle. She's my miracle, too."

Seven

Joel had briefly considered inviting Amy to the Hudsons' cookout. He'd thought it might be a good time to introduce her to his neighbors and announce their plans to marry. But he figured she didn't need the added pressure of meeting twenty new people and playing the happy bride-to-be. He was doubly glad he hadn't brought her when Debra arrived.

He watched as she approached, dressed in tight white jeans and silky black tank top. "I thought you had to work at the hospital tonight," he said.

"I switched shifts." She took his hand and smiled softly. "Besides, we haven't had a chance to see each other in weeks."

He gazed at her a long moment and then took a deep breath. He had to tell her about Amy. "We need to discuss some things."

She picked up on the edge in his voice. "Sounds serious. Should we do it now?"

"Yeah, I think we should."

They crossed the yard and entered his house through the screened-in porch. Just as Joel opened the door to the greatroom, Muffins streaked out and raced toward the screen door. She knew from experience that if she caught it before it latched, she could escape the confines of the house.

"Oh, damn!" Joel muttered as he lunged to catch the cat. He missed and Muffins disappeared outside. "I'll be back," he called as he gave chase.

Debra couldn't help laughing. Muffins loved this game and Joel wasn't quick enough to outsmart her. Debra was still smiling when the phone rang. She answered on the second ring.

There was a long pause before a hesitant voice said, "Is Joel there?"

"Well, he's here, but he's out trying to catch the cat right now. Can I have him return the call?"

"No, that's okay. Thank you." The line went dead, and Debra hung up.

"Who was that?" Joel asked as he tossed the cat onto the sofa.

"I don't know. She said she'd call later."

He nodded, guessing it was Amy and wondering what conclusions she was drawing about Debra answering his phone. He wasn't even sure Amy cared if a woman answered his phone.

Debra came to him and slid her arms around his waist. "Now what was so important?"

He looked at her and felt like a real idiot. They hadn't been together much in the past two months. Since his night with Amy, he'd felt vaguely uneasy whenever he'd been out with Debra. But still, he hadn't ended the relationship. As far as Debra was concerned, their busy schedules had kept them apart. Now he found himself searching for the best way to tell her he was about to marry someone else. He decided the direct approach would have to do.

"I'm getting married next Saturday."

Her blue eyes widened and she stepped back. "What?"

"I'm getting married."

"Who's the lucky girl?"

"Amy Michaels."

"I see." She slid her hands into the pockets of her jeans. "Is she pregnant?"

"Yes, she is."

"Lucky guess. You sure it's your baby?"

"Positive."

She considered him a long moment. "Are you in love with her?"

"I don't know," he answered honestly, surprising her. "I've loved her since the day she was born. I'm having a hard time getting past the point of seeing her as the little girl next door."

"Well, you must have managed to get past that hang-up at least once."

He looked a little sheepish. "Yeah. I felt I owed you an explanation."

She smiled grimly. "Maybe the little girl next door is the reason I could never get you past the hand-holding stage. Maybe your feelings for her are deeper than you think."

He shrugged. "Maybe you're right. Time will tell, I guess."

"Yeah." She reached up and touched his cheek. "Good luck, Joel. I hope you're happy."

"Thank you." He bent and kissed her cheek.

She walked to the door and stopped to look back at him over her shoulder. "I think that was Amy on the phone earlier. You should call her back." Without waiting for a reply, she opened the door and was gone.

He reached for the phone.

Joel lifted Amy's trembling left hand and slid the simple gold band onto her finger. She stared down at it, stunned by the magnitude of meaning attached to the thin circle of metal. Was it really possible that she was standing in a dingy paneled room listening to a dour-faced man recite her wedding ceremony? And had that really been her voice promising to love, honor, and cherish?

Tears stung her eyes. Everything seemed to be slightly out of focus, as if it were all a bad dream and she would wake up any minute now.

The only flowers present were in the small posy her mother had handed her just before the ceremony. There was no music, only a continuous hum of traffic outside the window. She was shaking and couldn't seem to control it.

From somewhere in the distance, she heard the rumpled Justice of the Peace pronounce them husband and wife. Panic seized her. What had she done? She should never have agreed to this. It was all a huge mistake.

Gentle fingers touched her cheek, and she looked up into Joel's face. He stood beside her, strong and solid, as usual. Hadn't he always been there for her when she needed him most? He was here now, and for a moment she felt safe and secure. And then the dark side of her mind reminded her that he was here out of obligation, not love.

Joel bent toward her and sealed the vows with a brush of his lips against hers. He'd watched the complicated emotions pass through her solemn eyes. Would he ever be able to find a way to make everything right between them? Or was he only fooling himself . . . and her?

Amy stood in the great-room and twisted the gold band on her finger. This was her home now. Joel was her husband. Surely this all an elaborate joke.

But her car was parked in his garage and her clothes hung in the master bedroom closet. She would eat her meals in his kitchen, shower in his bathroom, and sleep in his bed.

The last thought brought such a strong surge of panic to the surface that she felt dizzy. She closed her eyes and took a deep breath. She didn't need to be afraid. This was Joel. He wouldn't hurt her.

"Are you okay?"

Her eyes flew open, and the source of her discomfort stood a few feet away. Involuntarily, she took a step back. "I'm fine."

She saw the pain jump into his eyes before he turned

away. "You don't have to be afraid of me, Amy. I'm not going to hurt you. I promise." He shrugged out of his jacket and tossed it across the back of a chair. Then he sat down and looked up at her. "Okay. Let's talk."

She felt foolish standing, so she went over and sat down on the sofa. "Okay," she said softly.

"I want you to feel at home here. If you've got things in storage that you want here, let me know. We'll go get them. If you want to change things around, we'll change them. If I do something that bugs you, let me know. I can change."

He was rewarded by a small smile. "As far as the important things go, you can have the master bedroom. I'll take one of the others."

He paused, waiting to gauge her reaction. Her gaze collided with his briefly and then she quickly looked away. "I should take one of the other rooms. It doesn't seem fair to run you out of your room."

"Well, my intentions aren't purely honorable." With that her gaze shot back to him, and he saw more curiosity than fear in her eyes. "Sooner or later we're going to end up in the master bedroom together."

"You seem very sure of that," she said softly.

He nodded and stood. "I am." He turned and picked up his jacket. "Did I mention that I'm very neat?"

"No, but I remember that you are."

"What about you?"

She shrugged. "Not particularly."

"I seem to remember that about you," he returned, with a grin. "Right now, I'm going to change my clothes and then I'm going to pop some popcorn and watch an old John Wayne movie. Would you care to join me?"

"I guess so."

"Good." He glanced at his watch. "Show time is in fifteen minutes."

She watched as he disappeared down the hallway. For a moment she pondered the irony of her situation. This was her wedding night and the highlight would be a John Wayne western and a bowl of popcorn. If she weren't feeling so miserable, she might have found some humor in the strange turn of events. As it was, all she could think was that the reality of her wedding day was about as far from her childhood dreams as she could possibly get.

Amy woke early on Sunday morning, snuggled down into the covers of the king-sized bed and caught a fleeting scent of Joel's aftershave on the bedspread. Something stirred deep inside at the thought of his new status in her life. He was her husband. He belonged to her. At least technically. But she knew he didn't love her the way she wanted to be loved. He cared about her and the life she carried inside. For now it would have to be enough.

She pushed the covers back and slipped out of bed. Twenty minutes later she left the room showered and dressed in black shorts and a red tee shirt. Her hair was still damp and cascaded wildly about her shoulders. Her face was scrubbed clean, and she was pleased that a bit of natural color had returned to her cheeks. Her morning sickness had subsided. She felt at least halfway human in the mornings. It was a great relief to be able to move without the constant nausea plaguing her.

She checked the front porch hoping that Joel subscribed to the Sunday paper. It was there, just as she'd expected. She carried the bundled paper into the kitchen and set about making a pot of coffee. It took her only a moment to find the coffee and cups. Joel was as organized in his kitchen as he was in the rest of his life. A few minutes later she carried a cup of the steaming brew and the newspaper out to the screened-in porch.

Joel found her there thirty minutes later when the smell of fresh brewed coffee finally worked its way into his subconscious. She was sitting at the patio table with the paper spread out all over the top. He liked the way she looked at home.

"You make good coffee." He stepped out to join her. "I like that in a woman."

She looked up at him and felt as if something suddenly slammed into her chest. He wore black jogging shorts and nothing else. His hair was mussed, and an overnight beard covered his jaw and chin.

He sat down and began to dig through the scattered paper. "Okay," he muttered. "You make a great cup of coffee, but you mutilate the Sunday paper. I guess I can live with that."

"It's just a little messy. I would have straightened it up when I was done."

"Susan used to say that, too. I used to get up before her just so I could have the paper first. The comics and sports just weren't the same after she went through them."

"Poor baby," Amy crooned as she searched for the sports section and comics. She handed them over.

He leaned back in his chair and grinned. "Thanks." His blue eyes studied her. "Did you sleep okay?"

She nodded. "Just fine. I feel pretty good this morning."

"I thought so. You've actually got some color in your cheeks. I haven't seen that in a long time."

"Well, I think the morning sickness is winding down."

"When do you see the doctor again?"

She thought a moment. "I'll have to check my calendar."

"You've been putting in long hours at work, haven't you?" This was a subject he'd wanted to ask her about, but had refrained from doing so.

"I have to, Joel. I've got a lot to do."

"Maybe you should slow down a little."

She looked indignant. "I've been sick as a dog since the day I took this job. Now that I feel better I'm not going to slow down."

"You've been under a lot of strain both emotionally and physically. It's bound to catch up with you."

"I'm fine."

"Just promise me you'll take care of yourself."

"I'm not a child, Joel. I think I can take care of myself."

Amy stalked off into the house, and he stayed put. She'd reacted just as he'd expected. He had to trust her to be smart enough to know when to slow down. Yet he knew from experience that Amy tended to push herself to the limits.

He went in search of her a few minutes later and found her in the kitchen slamming through the cabinets. "What are you looking for?" he asked calmly.

"Don't you have a toaster?"

"In the pantry." He pointed at the door to her right.

She jerked the door open and looked around the well stocked closet. "Good grief. It looks like a grocery store in here."

"Is that a problem?"

"Maybe," she mumbled as she located the toaster on a bottom shelf. She set it on the counter and plugged it in, then turned to him. "Bread?"

"Try the fridge."

"I hate cold bread." She pulled the loaf out and continued to peer into the refrigerator. "Do you have any apple butter?"

"No, but I have some of my mom's strawberry jam."

She spotted it on the side shelf. "That'll do."

He winced as she slammed the door and walked back to the toaster. "Can we call a truce before you destroy the kitchen?"

She dropped the bread into the two slots and pushed the lever down forcefully before turning to him. "Don't think you can start telling me what to do," she warned bluntly.

"I wasn't trying to."

"I've managed on my own quite nicely. I don't need a keeper now."

"I'm not trying to be. But I do have a stake in your well-being."

"Only because I've let you." The bread popped up, and she plucked it gingerly from the toaster.

"What's that supposed to mean?" His voice was low, with a definite edge to it.

She started to spread the jam on the toast and didn't turn to him. "It means that I could have stayed in Kansas City and dealt with this situation on my own. I didn't have to let you know."

"You considered doing that?"

"Yes. You wouldn't even have known I was pregnant. I could have told you this was someone else's baby, and you would have willingly accepted it as the truth."

He caught her arm and swung her around to face him. His eyes turned cold as he looked down into her face.

She twisted her arm free and stepped back. "Don't look so shocked, Joel. There are a lot of ways to deal with an unwanted pregnancy. *I* thought about all of them, and *I* decided what was best for me. You have no right to act so self-righteous. You walked away from me and weren't planning to look back."

Her words hurt like hell because there was some truth to them. He'd made a royal error in judgment, and now he was paying the price. He knew if Amy ever trusted him again, it would be a long time in coming.

"I've got to get ready for work," he said flatly. "I'm holding an open house this afternoon, so I won't be back until around six."

He walked out of the room, and she turned back to the counter and two pieces of cold toast. She pressed a hand against her mouth trying to stifle the sob that threatened to escape.

Amy and Susan stood in the wallpaper section of the paint store and looked through every book, searching for the perfect nursery print.

"This is neat," Susan said, pointing to a blue paper with little baseball players all around the edge.

Amy frowned. "You can't put that up. What if you have a girl?"

"Brad says it's going to be a boy."

Amy looked at her blankly. "He's not psychic? Are you going to buy everything blue?"

Susan shook her head as she turned to the next selection. "No, of course not. But Brad really wants a boy. He grew up with three sisters." She stopped at another page. "I think this would work for either, don't you?"

The neutral design of dancing teddy bears was suitable for either a girl or boy. "Yeah, I like that a lot."

"Has Joel said anything about what he'd like your baby to be?" Susan slid a look at Amy.

"No. Do you like this one?" She pointed to the page in front of her although she didn't particularly like the paper. She just felt it was necessary to steer Susan away from the topic she had just introduced.

Amy was painfully aware that she and Joel had not talked about their baby in the same sense that most expectant parents do. They didn't talk about whether it would be a boy or a girl. They didn't pore over the name books and try them out on each other. They didn't dream of what their child would grow up to be.

"Too busy. The kid won't be able to sleep."

"You're probably right." Amy turned the page and knew she'd found the paper she wanted. Pastel rainbows and fluffy clouds with sleepy little angels. She ran her fingertips lightly over the paper and thought of the tiny life inside her. A part of her and Joel. An angel sent to them to care for.

"Are you going to get that?" Susan asked as she closed the book she'd been looking at. "It's pretty."

"I think I will. The small bedroom would make a good nursery."

Susan smiled. "Now you're talking. Tell you what. I'll help you put it up."

Joel arrived home late in the afternoon to find his wife and sister knee deep in wallpaper, and struggling. Amy was trying to get it straight at the top, while Susan was trying to accomplish the same thing at the bottom.

He leaned against the door frame and was immediately struck by the difference in the two women. Susan was just beginning to show, her rounded stomach slightly visible beneath the loose tee shirt she wore. Amy, on the other hand, was dressed in jeans with her cotton shirt neatly tucked inside the narrow waistband.

He knew that she had put on a few of the pounds she had lost early in her pregnancy. But she still looked pale and frail next to the glowing Susan, who had not experienced the slightest discomfort in these early months.

"This looks like a Laurel and Hardy routine," he teased.

Susan straightened, and Amy turned at the same moment. The paper, now unhindered, crumpled to the floor.

"I thought you had it," Amy said wearily.

"Well, I thought you had it," Susan returned. She let out a disgusted breath and sat down on the carpeting. "I'm tired. This is too much trouble. I thought all you had to do was get it wet and then slap it up there. I just don't think this paper is good."

Amy looked at Joel over Susan's head. She saw the laughter in his eyes and found herself hesitantly smiling back.

"Let me change, and I'll help you," he offered.

"Not me." Susan got up to go. "You and Amy can finish."

"When the going gets tough, Susan gets going," Joel remarked.

"You're so sweet." She pushed him out of the doorway. "Go away."

He grinned as he started down the hallway. "See you later, Susan."

"Goodbye, Joel," she called, sweetly sarcastic.

She watched as he disappeared into the spare bedroom. "Separate bedrooms?"

Amy shrugged and turned away from the concern in Susan's eyes. "It's no big deal. That's the way we want it for now."

"Oh, Amy," Susan whispered. "What are you two doing to each other?"

Amy's eyes flashed with rare temper. "Just leave it alone."

"I'm worried about you two. You're both acting so strange about this."

Amy felt uncharacteristic anger boil uncontrollably inside her. "Don't you get it, Susan? This is a gigantic mistake. The baby, the marriage, everything is a mistake. Joel and I should never have gotten married. He doesn't love me. And this baby should never have happened."

Susan was stunned. "You don't mean that."

"I mean every word. You don't understand, because you look at everything that's happening to you through love-colored eyes. I don't. I'm dealing in cold, hard reality here. Susan, I've never felt more trapped in my life."

"You and Joel can have a good life together. You've got such a solid foundation to build on."

Amy threw her hands up in mock surrender. "If it's so damned solid, then why did he turn away from me when I needed him most?"

"I don't know. Have you asked him?"

"He justifies it nicely, but he can't change the facts. If I hadn't bothered to tell him that I was pregnant, he'd never know, because he wouldn't have bothered asking."

Susan would never be convinced by that accusation. "He made a mistake . . ."

"Exactly," Amy snapped. "Just another mistake. It's incredible how many we've made. All our lives—mine, Joel's, and the baby's—are going to be so messed up there will be no hope of ever straightening things out."

"I can't believe how bitter you've become."

"You don't know what it's like to have your heart shattered by the one person you thought you could trust above all others."

Joel stepped out into the hallway and saw Susan still standing in the doorway to the smaller room. "Are you still hanging around?" he asked. His smile faded when she turned somber blue eyes to him. "What is it?"

She shook her head and said sadly, "I don't know either of you anymore." She turned and hurried down the hallway. Joel called her name, but the sound of the front door closing was the only answer he got.

He walked to the bedroom door and stopped within its frame. "What was that all about?"

Amy began to pick up the room. "Just a lesson in harsh reality."

Joel watched her a moment and then spoke very softly. "Are you so jealous of Susan's happiness that you feel the need to destroy it?"

Amy straightened, her back to him, and let his words sink in past the anger and pain. Susan had been trying to help, and she had viciously pushed her away.

Joel came to stand beside her and surveyed the work she and Susan had already done. He ran a hand over the new paper. "You guys did a pretty good job."

He looked at her then and saw the sorrow in her eyes. Reaching out hesitantly, he touched her cheek and was pleased that she didn't flinch. "Don't worry about it," he said gently. "Call her later. It'll be okay."

"I feel like I've just kicked a puppy."

Joel smiled at the simile. "I've felt that way a time or two myself over the years." He turned his attention back to the chore at hand. "Let's see if we can get this finished tonight."

Amy stood back, trying to envision the room completely prepared for a baby. Her baby. She brought a hand to her still-flat stomach and held it there. Inside a new life grew— a life totally dependent on her. Joel had helped with the creating, but it was up to her to nurture and care for the tiny being. She felt a twinge of guilt.

Susan was right. She had become bitter and had been blaming the only innocent party involved. This child had not asked to be created. She and Joel had made that decision on their own.

She looked at Joel's back as he smoothed out a newly pasted sheet of paper. Quietly, she spoke his name, and he turned to look at her over his shoulder. He tensed, seeing tears on her cheeks, and quickly crossed the room to her.

"What is it?" he asked, concern lacing his words.

"I'm sorry about the way I've been acting."

His eyes softened. He felt as if his heart was expanding inside his chest. "It's okay. I know this has been hard for you."

"I really do want this baby, Joel."

"I know you do." He reached up and traced one of her tears with a fingertip. "I do, too."

"I've been so selfish. I've been blaming the baby for something he had no choice in. I feel awful."

"Amy." Tenderly he framed her face with his hands, finding great pleasure in the chance to touch her. "You can't blame yourself for your feelings. You've had a lot to deal with these last few weeks, and I haven't helped much. Don't start beating up on yourself now."

She reached up and took hold of his hand. Slowly, she brought it down to rest on her stomach. "We created the life growing inside here. It wasn't a mistake. It's our miracle."

Sweet emotion welled up within him. He looked down

at their joined hands and wondered if his knees were capable of holding him up much longer. He lifted his gaze to hers. "I'm not sorry," he whispered.

She shook her head and stepped closer. Instinctively, his arms slid around her, drawing her to him. She rested her head on his shoulder. He closed his eyes as true contentment flooded him. Amy was coming home.

Eight

Amy's attention drifted from the computer screen to the scene outside her window. Her office overlooked the courtyard, and already the trees overshadowing the benches and picnic tables were beginning to show a hint of changing colors amid the green leaves. October was fast approaching, and soon cooler temperatures and shorter days would prevail. Amy hated seeing the golden days of summer pass.

She shifted her attention back to the terminal and stiffened as a sharp pain pierced her lower back. That was the third time she'd felt the strange sensation since lunch. She'd have to remember to mention it to the doctor when she saw him tomorrow.

She checked her watch. It was nearly six, and she was tired. After a moment of indecision, she decided to call it a day. She saved the current copy of her report and then turned the computer off. She'd get in early in the morning and finish it before the board meeting.

She pushed her chair back and stood. Startled, she clutched the edge of the desk as the world around her began to dip at a strange angle. Closing her eyes, she waited for the dizziness to pass. She'd better mention this to the doctor, too.

The drive home was uneventful, and she sighed with appreciation as she kicked off her heels and dropped her briefcase beside the sofa. She stopped and rubbed Muffins under the chin. "Something smells great."

"Dinner in ten minutes," Joel called from the kitchen. "Go take a look in the nursery."

She padded down the hall in stocking feet. In the corner sat a wooden rocking horse, complete with a painted red saddle and a mane and tail of black yarn. She walked over and bent to touch the smooth wood.

"Do you like it?" Joel asked from the doorway.

"It's wonderful. Where did you get it?"

"Valley Mall. I passed that shop called Country Charm and there was Buster sitting out front."

Amy laughed and looked at him over her shoulder. "Buster?"

"I think Buster is a great name for a horse. He likes it."

She looked back at the smiling horse. "I guess he does," she murmured. "He's a nice touch."

"Well, I thought the room needed something more." He shrugged. "Buster is a start."

They hadn't done anything more since they'd finished papering two weeks ago. The wooden horse was the first real addition to the room.

"I've got Sunday free," Joel continued. "If you feel like it, I thought we might go out and buy some of the baby things we'll need."

Amy smiled, touched by the offer. "That sounds great." She moved to straighten and gasped as a searing pain shot through her back.

Joel was immediately beside her, reaching out to steady her. "Are you all right?" he asked anxiously, watching her closely.

She nodded as the pain faded. "I'm okay now."

"What was that?"

"Just a random pain. Nothing to worry about."

He didn't release her, and she was acutely aware of the scent of his aftershave and his closeness. "Have you had the pain before?" he asked.

"Just once or twice this afternoon. I'll mention them to the doctor tomorrow when I go in."

"Are you sure we shouldn't call him now?"

She shook her head. "I'm okay, Joel."

"Amy." He spoke her name softly, and she looked up into blue eyes shaded dark with worry. When he bent toward her, she responded instinctively by tilting her head so that his mouth easily found hers. The first touch was tentative, a testing of emotional waters.

Her arms slid upward around his neck, and her fingers tangled in his hair. The kiss deepened and lit the fuse of desire long ignored, yet highly volatile.

Amy reveled in the feel of his body pressed against hers and drifted back to a perfect night of love shared a lifetime ago. She remembered every detail, every nuance. The restless yearning in her demanded that she take what could so easily be hers. But the pragmatic side of her nature whispered that she needed more than the physical love being offered. She needed this man to love her totally, with his heart, mind, body, and soul.

Joel felt her easing away and nearly groaned at the thought of releasing her. Holding her now, feeling her response, nearly drove him beyond the edge of reason. Their one night together couldn't have been an illusion. Not when he felt this fire racing through his blood.

He opened his eyes and stared down into hers. There was passion and desire and a wariness that caused him to pause. Until he could win her trust, the wariness would stay. He wanted it gone when they finally made love.

Joel let go, reluctantly. "Do you have any idea what you do to me?"

She laughed softly. "I had a pretty good idea when you were holding me close."

He liked the mischievous light in her eyes. It reminded him of the woman he'd fallen in love with.

The unbidden thought nearly knocked him off his feet.

When had it happened? When had all the confusion eased and the fear faded? Had his love for her just crept into his heart and waited patiently for his mind to catch up?

"Joel, are you okay?"

She was looking at him as if he'd just taken leave of his senses. For all he knew, maybe he had. But he didn't think so. Loving Amy, body and soul, seemed like a very natural thing to do.

He nearly told her, then stopped himself. Blurting it out wouldn't do. He'd have to make her understand that what he was feeling was real, and had nothing to do with fulfilling his obligations, but everything to do with her.

"Joel, you're acting really weird."

He pulled himself together and grinned. "Sorry. Let's eat." He turned abruptly and left the room whistling a cheery tune.

Joel jerked awake and stared into the darkness, an uneasiness stealing over him.

He rolled to his side and sat up as he rubbed a hand over his face. He pulled on a pair of jogging shorts, and started from the room without turning on the lights.

He flipped on the hall light and blinked against the glaring brightness and the horror of the scene it revealed. All vestiges of sleep fled instantly, and his heart kicked into triple time. Amy lay on her side at his feet.

He knelt beside her and gently turned her onto her back. Blood oozing from a gash on her forehead contrasted sharply against her deathly pale skin. His hand shook as he searched for a pulse and found it, faint but steady.

"You're going to be all right, sweetheart," he whispered as he stood and rushed back into the bedroom to call an ambulance. He jerked on a tee shirt and tennis shoes as he gave the necessary information. When he hung up, he went to the front door, turned on all the outside lights and left the door open.

He raced back to Amy and dropped down beside her. "Everything's okay, honey. You're going to be . . ." His voice faltered as his gaze scanned her body. "Oh, God," he groaned. The deep scarlet stain spreading at the hem of her cotton nightgown could only be from one source.

He bent close to her, his trembling hand caressing her cheek. "Amy, I love you. Please hear me. I need for you to know. You've got to be okay so I can tell you every day how much I love you. You can't leave me now."

The distant wail of a siren drifted eerily in the night air. Joel listened a moment and then gathered her into his arms. The ambulance pulled into the driveway at the same instant he emerged from the house. Within minutes they were headed back toward the hospital.

Joel followed behind as they rushed her into the emergency room, and a crew of white-clad professionals surrounded her. A hand on his arm caught his attention, and he turned to look into the face of a sympathetic young nurse.

"Sir, you can't go in there," she said kindly. "If you'll come with me, I'll show where you can clean up, and then I'll need to get some information from you." Joel looked at her blankly, then down. The life that had drained out of Amy now stained his hands and arms.

Anne watched her son pace the length of the cheerfully decorated waiting room. She was certain he was close to wearing a path in the blue carpeting. Back and forth he went, the same number of steps each time, the same rhythm.

He'd called her just after four A.M. and she'd come right away, stopping only to pick up a clean shirt and jeans for him.

Amy's condition was unknown. Joel had brought her in nearly two hours ago, and the doctors were still with her.

Anne's attention was drawn to the doorway as Neil and Brenda entered. The two women's eyes met across the room, and a shared compassion passed between them. Neil went to Joel, and the younger man stopped his pacing long enough to fill them in on what little he knew. Simply put, there was nothing to do but wait.

Twenty minutes later, the same nurse that had taken the insurance information stepped into the doorway "Mr. Hartman?"

Joel swung around. "Yes. How is she?"

"Your wife is stable and resting right now. Dr. Rowland will be in to see you in a few minutes."

"Thank you." He was too keyed up to sit. Too afraid to be still.

Images of Amy flashed in his mind. Why hadn't he heard her get up? She must have known something was wrong and had come to get him. He suspected she'd fallen in the hallway and struck her head on the doorknob of the linen closet.

He remembered the pain she'd experienced in the nursery the evening before and silently swore. Why hadn't he insisted that she call the doctor right then and there instead of waiting for her appointment?

The man who entered the room was tall, late forties, and dressed casually in wrinkled tan slacks and a striped brown shirt. "Mr. Hartman?" He extended his hand. "I'm Ted Rowland, Amy's doctor."

"Can I see her?"

"Yes. I'll take you to her room in a moment." His gaze shifted to include the three other people, whom he assumed to be the parents, standing anxiously behind the young husband.

"We couldn't save the pregnancy. I'm sorry." He saw the flash of raw pain in Joel's eyes. "A spontaneous abortion, or a miscarriage, at this stage usually happens because something is vitally wrong with the fetus. Amy lost a lot of blood. She'll be weak, but there was no internal damage. Amy should have no problem conceiving again, although I would prefer that she wait awhile before trying again.

"As far as the cut on her forehead goes, we closed it up with eight stitches. She regained consciousness before I left her, and her vital signs and reflexes were good. I don't anticipate any problems, but I want her to stay until tomorrow. Do you have any questions?"

"Can I see her?" Joel asked, his voice hushed.

The doctor's smile was filled with compassion. He knew that little of what he'd just explained had really sunk in. "Come with me."

Joel pulled a chair close to Amy's bed and dropped into it. He sat for a long time and just stared at her. The cut on her forehead had been stitched carefully, but a bruise had formed around it. He saw that her hands rested on her stomach, as if, even in sleep, she could protect the life that had ceased to exist there. Another piece of his heart cracked.

He reached over and covered her left hand with his. "I'm sorry," he whispered, drawing the limp fingers to his lips. "So very sorry." With great care he cradled her hand between both of his, wanting to warm her, needing to reach her.

Amy struggled through a misty whirlpool of light and sound until she managed to force her eyes open. She was aware of the intense pain in her head and a vague feeling of overwhelming loss. She tried to lift her left hand and found it immobile. Slowly, her eyes focused, and she realized Joel was clutching her hand between his own.

She spoke his name softly, and he lifted his head. Their eyes met and held. She saw the despair in his eyes, the tears on his cheeks, and felt her own spill over in response.

* * *

Anne drove Joel home late in the morning. They entered the house through the garage and were met by the mournful meow of Muffins, who had been without food far too long for her comfort. Joel immediately fed her and then went to the nursery. Anne followed.

"Mom, I need for you to do me a favor."

She stepped into the room and frowned as he stripped the first piece of paper from the wall. "Joel, what are you doing?"

"Buy some new paper, okay? Anything will do. If you go to the store now, I could repaper it before I go back to the hospital tonight."

"Honey, you're exhausted. You can't possibly do this whole room today."

The sound of tearing paper filled the room. "Yes, I can. If I get started right away."

Anne recognized the contained fury in the way he ripped the paper from the wall. "Changing this room isn't going to change what's happened," she said quietly.

"I know that. I just don't want Amy to come home and be reminded by it."

"She should make the decision to change it. You can't hide all the traces and pretend it never happened."

He grew very still, then drew an unsteady breath and turned to face her. "I don't know what to do," he admitted wearily. "I've done so many things wrong with Amy. I just don't want to hurt her anymore."

"I understand that, Joel, but you lost something precious. Amy may need to remember."

"I should have known something was wrong. She said she had some pain yesterday, but she didn't seemed concerned. I should have called the doctor."

"Joel, it won't help to blame yourself. Nothing you or Amy did or didn't do caused this to happen. There's no one to blame."

His gaze seemed to go through her, as if he were seeing

into some distant world, sadness stealing over his features. "She'll blame herself for everything."

"Then you've got to convince her that she's wrong."

"How?" He lifted his hands in a helpless gesture. "Mom, she's convinced that the only reason I married her was because of the baby. She doesn't know how much she means to me because I've never told her. She doesn't know how much I love her because I didn't know myself until yesterday, before this happened. If I tell her now, she's not going to believe me. I doubt that I can convince her of anything."

"She's been hurt. It's going to take awhile for her to heal. But if you two can work through this, you'll have a rock solid foundation to build on."

"And if we can't?"

"Then you'll be two miserable people." She took his hand and squeezed it. "Honey, I can't think of two people better suited to each other than you and Amy. But it's going to take time to get things straightened out."

Joel slid his arms around his mother and hugged her close. "Thanks for being here. My faith and logic both seem a little shaky right now."

Anne felt tears sting her eyes, but blinked them away. Stepping back, she looked up at him. "You're going to be okay," she assured him. "So will Amy. Just give yourselves the time you need." She turned then to survey the room. "Okay," she said briskly. "You've ruined some perfectly good paper."

"You really think I should leave it up?"

"I really do, Joel. At some point Amy's going to need to come in here. It may take days or even weeks, but I know what I'm talking about."

He considered her words, then looked at the damage he'd already done. "I guess I'd better go and get some paper to replace what I've torn off."

"I'll go for you. How much do I need?"

"One roll should do it."

She nodded and started toward the door.

"Will you do me one other favor?" he asked suddenly.

She paused and looked at him closely. "Whatever you need."

He bent and picked up the rocking horse. "If I put Buster in your car, will you give him a temporary home?"

Her smile was gentle. "Sure. I'll be glad to keep Buster until you're ready for him again."

Susan was determined that she wasn't going to cry. But her first glimpse of Amy was nearly her undoing. "Well," she said, her voice wavering, "you look a lot like you did when you ran your bicycle into the garage that summer we were twelve."

A trembling smile lifted Amy's mouth as she reached for Susan's hand. "I feel about the same way."

Susan bit her lip and squeezed the hand tightly. "I promised myself I wouldn't cry," she announced, even as two tears brimmed over and traced down her cheeks.

"Me, too." The laugh Amy tried for came out as a sob. "Oh, God, Susan. I've made such a mess of things."

"No, you haven't." Susan carefully wrapped her arms around her lifetime friend. "It's all going to be okay, honey. You'll see."

Amy's tears came from the innermost corners of her soul. Only Susan could understand the depth of her grief, and the pain and guilt that had come to settle around her heart.

When the emotional storm passed, Amy settled back into the pillows, physically spent, her head throbbing painfully. She kept hold of Susan's hand. "Have you seen Joel?" she asked, her voice raw.

Susan took a deep breath. "I stopped by to see him before I came here. He said he'd be by later."

"He was really upset this morning." Amy's voice caught

and she swallowed hard, remembering. "I've never seen him like that. Not even when your dad died."

"From what Mom told me, he was terrified. He loves you, Amy."

Amy's gaze dropped to their joined hands. "Like he loves you."

"No." Susan squeezed her friend's fingers, demanding her attention. "Not like me at all. I wish I could make you two talk to each other about what you're really feeling." She stood, too agitated to sit any longer.

"You know," she continued, "you've been so angry with him because of the way he treated you. But I think he acted that way because he was scared to death of what he was feeling for you." She stopped at the foot of Amy's bed. "I know my brother."

"I thought I knew him," Amy said thoughtfully. "I found out there was a lot I didn't know."

"Exactly!" Susan exclaimed as if Amy had just made a major discovery. "He's acting strange because he's never been in love before. He doesn't have a clue as to what he should be doing. Falling in love with you just about blew him away, Amy."

"You make everything sound so simple."

"It could be if you'd both let it." She paused a moment. "What are you going to do tomorrow when you're released?"

"Mom and Dad want me to go home for a while."

"Are you going?"

"I think so."

"Do you mind if I state my opinion here?"

A semblance of a smile curved Amy's mouth. "Have I ever been able to stop you from stating anything?"

"No." There was no laughter in Susan's blue eyes. "I think you're making a mistake by going to your parents. Your home is with Joel now."

Amy hesitated, then spoke carefully. "Susan, I know you

mean well, but I have to decide how I feel about Joel. We can easily have the marriage annulled."

"You can't do that," Susan said quietly. "You and Joel have so much to offer each other."

"Maybe we did. I'm not so sure now."

"I just want one promise from you. Don't rush into any decision. Give yourself, and Joel, time to work things out."

Amy shrugged helplessly. "I don't know what I want to do. I need some time to think things through. I think that will be easier for me if I'm away from him."

Susan walked around the edge of the bed and bent to kiss Amy's cheek. "Whatever happens," she said gently, "I want you to know that it won't change our friendship. I love you, Amy, no matter what."

Susan saw fresh tears gather in Amy's eyes and quickly stepped back from the bed. "Oh, no," she groaned. "I can't handle any more tears. I'm leaving right now. I'll call you tomorrow."

"You'd better leave. I'm going to drown if you don't."

Susan managed a smile and left.

Joel stared at his wife a long, intense moment before turning to look out the window. Amy shifted in the bed. She recognized the angry tension in his stance, but she'd also seen pain in his eyes before he'd turned away.

"Try to see my side, Joel," she pleaded softly. "All I'm asking for is time to think."

"We need to work things out together." He continued to stare out the window, seeing nothing of the busy world outside.

"Eventually, maybe. But not just yet. I need to be alone for a while."

He closed his eyes, giving in to the exhaustion that he had been fighting for hours. He felt as if he'd run a very long race at top speed and still come in last.

"I just want to know something." His voice reflected the weariness weighing him down. "Was this your idea or your parents'?"

"It was their suggestion."

He turned toward her then, and she saw a tumult of emotion in his eyes and a bone-deep fatigue she hadn't noticed earlier. "Are you going to follow their advice when they suggest you have this marriage annulled?"

The absolute defeat in his voice both surprised and unnerved her. She'd almost convinced herself that he would be relieved by her decision. Now she wasn't so sure. "Joel, don't do this, please. Don't try to make them into the bad guys."

He slashed an impatient hand through his hair. "Okay. You're right. I'm sorry." He walked to the foot of her bed. "Do what you have to do, Amy."

He walked to the door, reached for the handle, then stopped. Taking a deep breath and drawing on every ounce of courage he had, he swung back around to face her. "I have this strange feeling that if I don't tell you this now, I may never have another chance." He paused, his blue eyes clear and bright with emotion she'd never seen before. "I love you, Amy. In more ways than I can count and in more ways than I ever thought possible. When you're working things out, keep that in mind."

Nine

"Good morning, Joel! It's another beautiful day!" Even Stacy Miles's effervescence couldn't lift Joel's somber mood.

"Good morning," he called back, the enthusiasm obviously lacking from his voice.

Stacy stuck her head into his office. "Why the long face? It's a great day. Opportunity is out there just waiting for someone to grab it. I plan on being that someone." She leaned back against the doorjamb looking very pleased with herself. For two years she had been his top producing agent. She had drive and ambition, with a natural business sense thrown in.

A small smile touched his mouth as he looked at her. "Have you been listening to motivational tapes again?"

"No." She smiled smugly. "I don't need tapes when I can sell a property like this." She crossed the distance to his desk to offer him a legal size manila folder.

Joel looked inside, and he gave a low whistle. "Wow. I get your point." Displayed before him was an accepted purchase agreement on a very expensive piece of property.

"I told you I'd sell it. My listing and my buyers make a fantastic commission. And I had the buyers go in to be pre-approved for financing before we wrote the offer. It's a done deal."

"Congratulations." Joel looked up, his smile genuine. "You've made yourself a nice little profit here."

"You bet I have. Don't forget your cut."

He chuckled softly. "The bills will be paid for at least another month."

"Ha! Try two."

"Do the sellers have to find something?"

Stacy nodded. "They want something in Meadow Lake. I'll see what's available, and we'll go looking this afternoon."

Joel leaned back in his chair. "Gee, you can quit for the rest of the year and still surpass what you made last year."

"No way! I'm just getting a taste of the big bucks. I'm not slowing down now."

The phone rang, and she dashed out to her desk to answer it. Joel looked back at the papers spread before him. The company was having a fantastic year profitwise, and Stacy had been a big part of it. He wished he could feel a little more excited. But a bone-deep loneliness had settled over him in the last few days that he couldn't seem to shake.

It had been just over a week since he'd seen Amy in the hospital. He'd lost count of how many times he'd reached for the phone to call her before stopping himself. She'd asked for time. As much as it hurt, he would give her that.

A soft knock at his door drew his attention. He was startled to see Brenda standing there. Rising, he said, "I'm sorry. I didn't hear you come in."

"I hope I'm not interrupting anything."

"No, of course not. Come in and have a seat."

She moved into the office and settled into a chair across from him. "I thought we ought to talk," she said.

"Okay." He sat back down behind the desk. "Is Amy okay?"

Brenda nodded. "She's feeling stronger every day." She smoothed her skirt in a nervous movement. "I want to thank you for giving her this time to work things out. Neil and I thought it would be best."

"I wasn't happy about her decision," he said evenly.

"I know you weren't. But you respected it. That's what's important."

"I have to be honest with you, Brenda. It's not easy for me to stay away. I love her very much."

Brenda studied him a long moment, as if searching for the truth behind his words. "I believe you do," she said finally, quietly. "But you always have."

He shook his head and leaned forward. "Not the way I do now. If I have to start all the way back at square one, I will. We've got too much to lose now."

A smile lit the older woman's face. "You've always been determined to get what you want."

She paused and took a deep breath. "You don't need to worry about Amy. She loves you, too."

"I'm going to make her happy, Brenda," he vowed. "I want you and Neil to understand that. I've made plenty of stupid mistakes with her, but I'm going to take care of all that. When I found her in the hallway that morning, I felt panic like nothing I've ever felt before. I would have bargained with Satan himself if I'd had to. She means that much to me."

Brenda nodded, trusting the sincerity she heard in his voice. "How have you been the last week?" she asked gently. "I know it's been hard for you, too."

He swallowed hard against unexpected emotion. "There will be other children for us."

She nodded and pushed to her feet. "I won't keep you any longer. I just wanted to stop by and check on you."

"Thank you." He came around the desk to her. Without hesitation they shared a hug. "Tell Amy I miss her," he whispered against her hair.

Brenda stepped back and nodded. "Give her a little longer, Joel. It'll be worth it." A smile crept into her eyes. "In the meantime, I'll keep you posted."

"It's a deal." He walked her to the door and watched as

she drove away. After her visit the day didn't seem nearly as dismal.

"I saw Joel this morning."

The late afternoon sun cast long shadows along the quiet country road, doing little to dispel the autumn chill in the air. Amy tucked her hands into the pockets of her blue sweatshirt.

"How was he?" she asked after feeling her mother's curious eyes on her.

"He looked a little tired but seemed okay. He misses you."

Amy sighed and kicked restlessly at a stone in the middle of road. "Why did you go see him?"

"I was worried about him. I wanted to see for myself that he was okay."

Amy looked over at her mother, her amber eyes shaded with emotion. "I don't know what to do about Joel, Mom."

"How do you feel about him?"

Amy was unable to answer for a moment. "I love him. But I'm not sure I can pick up married life as if nothing happened."

"I don't think he'd pressure you. Why don't you talk to him?"

Amy shook her head. "I don't know. Maybe I'm just crazy. I feel like we ought to go back and touch some of the bases we missed. Like dating and stuff like that. I mean, we've never even been out to a movie and dinner together. I don't know what his dreams are for the future. I always thought I knew everything about him. But now I realize I don't know him very well at all." She frowned at her mother. "Am I making any sense to you?"

Brenda chuckled softly and slipped an arm around her daughter's shoulders. "Actually, yes. I understand how you feel."

"Good. Then I'm not crazy."

"Far from it. Why don't you talk to Joel? Tell him what you just told me. I think he'll try to understand. You may even find that he feels the same way."

Amy looked at her with hopeful eyes. "Do you really think so?"

"Amy, the man loves you. I think he'd agree to anything that would bring you two together. Just give him the chance."

A comfortable silence stretched between them as they continued their stroll. As they rounded the curve, the Radley farmhouse came into view. The trees flanking the dingy white building displayed more orange leaves than green, and a gust of wind sent a shower of color drifting to the ground.

Amy stopped and gazed up at the graceful lines of the Victorian structure. "Why doesn't someone buy that house? It's a shame to see it deteriorate. Were you ever in it?"

"No. James Radley pretty much kept to himself. He was in his seventies when your dad and I moved here."

"I wish there was some way to buy it. I wouldn't want all the land, of course, but the house could be fantastic with some work."

"Well, your dad wanted to buy the land bordering our property line but found that the whole estate is tied up in legal proceedings. The heirs are bickering over something."

Amy shivered as the wind sent leaves dancing around their feet. "Joel thinks it will probably be sold to developers."

"Unfortunately, he's probably right."

Amy turned away and started back toward home. She couldn't bear the thought of the house being torn down to make room for a housing development. She also couldn't explain her attraction to the old place, but it was something she'd felt her entire life.

* * *

Amy was glad when the doctor released her to return to work the following week. The cut on her forehead had healed neatly. The stitches had been removed, and the scar was barely noticeable under her hair. The emotional scars left from the miscarriage were healing at a much slower pace, however. If she hadn't allowed herself to get so upset, if she'd taken better care of herself, if she'd forgiven Joel instead of holding a grudge . . .

In her darkest moods, the list went on and on. Yet she knew what the doctor had told her was true. Mother Nature had merely done what was necessary.

Late at night, in the solitude of her room, Amy allowed herself to dream of another child. One with blond hair and bright blue eyes, always smiling and brimming with sweetness. A child with Joel's humor and her curiosity. A child conceived within a solid and loving relationship.

She hadn't seen or spoken to Joel since he'd left her hospital room. But his parting words were branded in her mind. She didn't doubt that he meant what he said.

It was her hope that the time they were spending apart would help them discover how much of what they felt was real and how much was attached to the pregnancy. For herself, the answer was crystal clear. She'd fallen in love with Joel before she'd gotten pregnant. That love may have been battered in the past few weeks, but it was very much there, surviving still.

Amy was greeted by a computer generated banner welcoming her back to her office. It had been signed by many of her coworkers, some she hadn't even met yet.

"Welcome back." Mark came in behind her. "We missed you."

"Thank you." She turned and set her briefcase down beside the desk. "I'm glad to be back." She noticed the neat stacks of paperwork on her desk and made a face. "I think."

"There's no hurry. Don't push yourself."

She moved behind her desk and looked across at him. "I want to thank you again for presenting my report at the board meeting."

"No problem. The board members understood."

She nodded. "Good. Hopefully, I'll be in better form next month."

"You'll be fine." He hesitated a moment. "I'm sorry about the miscarriage."

She returned his gaze steadily. "How did you find out? No one knew I was pregnant."

"When I called the hospital to check on you, the nurse told me. After she said it I think she realized her mistake. She wouldn't give me any more information. I was able to put the pieces together after that. Things began to make better sense."

Amy frowned. "What things?"

Mark slid his hands into the pockets of his pleated pants and gave a soft laugh. "It's interesting the things that stay with you. I remember you telling me once that you wanted a big wedding with all the trimmings. You also wanted a romantic honeymoon on some warm, far-off island. I had a hard time understanding why you'd get married on a Saturday afternoon with only your family present. Especially when you were twenty-six and marrying a man you've known your whole life." He shook his head slowly. "I don't know why, but I never considered you might be pregnant."

"Life is real funny sometimes, isn't it, Mark?" Her smile was rueful. "When we were young and in love we consciously chose not to risk a teenage pregnancy." She shrugged. "Joel and I didn't even stop to think. Just goes to show that wisdom doesn't necessarily come with age."

"Do you love him?"

"I've loved him forever, will love him forever."

"That's how I feel about Julie."

"I'm glad," Amy agreed quietly. They looked at one an-

other, each marveling at the totally different journeys they'd
taken to arrive at exactly the same point.

Mark shook his head and turned toward the door. "I better get out of here so you can get started. Don't overdo,"
he warned gently.

"I promise I won't."

"Good. I'll see you later."

She stared at the empty doorway a moment longer and
then sighed as her gaze returned to her desk. She had a lot
of catching up to do.

Amy juggled the file folders in her arms and glanced
down at her watch as she stepped off the elevator. It was
twelve-fifteen, and she was starving. For the first time in
weeks, the thought of food actually appealed to her. Pizza
sounded wonderful. She rounded the corner into her office
and came to an abrupt halt, the files nearly sliding out of
her arms.

Joel turned from the window at the sound of her entrance.
Across the room, their eyes met and held, each searching.
She thought he looked a little worn around the edges, but
wonderful in spite of it.

"Hi," he said quietly. He shifted uncomfortably, sliding
his hands into his pockets. She sensed his uneasiness and
was surprised by it.

"Hi," she returned as she walked over to place the files
on her desk. She turned back to face him, a few feet of
open space between them. "It's good to see you."

The relief he felt at her words was clearly visible. "I
couldn't stay away any longer."

"I'm not upset," she assured him gently. "How have you
been?"

"I've managed. You look great." He meant it. The pale
blue sweater she wore only emphasized the healthy glow of
her skin. She looked rested and relaxed and more like his

Amy. "You can barely see the place on your forehead. How are you feeling?"

"Okay. Happy to be back at work."

He nodded. "Good. I'm glad." His gaze lingered on her face. It was all he could do not to reach for her. He'd felt so alone these last two weeks. It was almost laughable. He'd never known loneliness before Amy.

She opened a bottom drawer of her desk and took her purse out. "It's lunchtime, and I'm starving." She smiled at him. "Wanna buy me lunch?"

He felt as if a huge weight had just been lifted from his shoulders. "I'd love to."

They walked three blocks and shared a pizza at a little shop that catered to the lunchtime crowd by providing fast service and good food. When they finished and stepped back out into the crisp October air, Amy reached for Joel's hand.

"Let's go this way," she said, tugging him in the opposite direction of her office. "Let's see what's happening on the Circle."

He smiled and gladly followed her. They walked along Market Street, toward the Soldiers and Sailors Monument dominating the horizon. Amy liked the way Lady Victory reached high into the crystal blue sky. The large stone sculptures surrounding the monument, along with pools of cascading water, never ceased to impress her.

Beneath a canopy of a clear autumn sky, Amy and Joel headed back toward her office. When he stopped and disappeared inside one of the small shops, Amy watched through the window as he made his purchase. Moments later he came back out and presented it to her.

She took the bouquet of pink and white carnations and smiled up at him. At that moment it didn't matter that people crowded around them and time ticked away. She was lost in blue eyes shining with love meant only for her. She reached for his hand, and they walked the few blocks back to her office.

When they reached her building, Joel released her hand and slid his own into his pockets. "I won't go in," he said.

"Okay. Thanks for lunch and the flowers."

He nodded. "You're welcome." He looked at her a long moment, then took a step backward. "I better get going."

"Yeah, me, too." She started to turn away from him but felt her gaze drawn back to his as if by magnetic force. She looked into his eyes and saw all the dreams she'd ever longed for and all the promises she'd ever need. Her past and her future came together in this one man.

With great effort she pulled her gaze away and turned to go inside. Neither of them said goodbye, and as she rode the elevator to her floor, doubt began to gnaw at her with a vengeance.

They hadn't talked about anything important over lunch. What if he'd decided in the last two weeks that he didn't really love her, but he just didn't know how to tell her?

The bell pinged at her floor, and the doors of the elevator slid open with a quiet swish. Amy stepped out and started down the hall toward her office. She had just stepped inside the door when the telephone began to ring. She lifted the receiver and answered.

"I forgot to tell you something important."

Joel's voice had a sudden, instantaneous impact on her pulse. Her hand gripped the receiver so tightly that her knuckles turned white. All she could say was a breathless, "Yes?"

"I love you, Amy. More than you know."

"Oh, Joel." Tears sprang to her eyes. How easily he turned her world upside down!

"Can I see you tomorrow night? Maybe dinner and a movie?"

Amy bit her lip and blinked away the tears clinging to her lashes. "Yes, I'd like that."

"Good." She could hear his sigh of relief over the line. "I'll pick you up at six."

"Okay. I'll see you then."

"You won't forget?"

She smiled, wondering how he could ask such a silly question. "I won't forget. I promise."

"Okay. I'll see you later. Bye."

"Bye," she echoed, slowly replacing the receiver. She reached down and picked up one perfect carnation, bringing its soft, pink petals to her cheek.

"Mom, how does this look?"

Brenda turned from the stove to look at her daughter. Amy was dressed in jeans and a pink cable knit sweater that skimmed loosely over her hips to mid-thigh. Her hair was pulled up at the sides and swung freely across her shoulders.

"You might want to consider shoes," Brenda suggested blandly.

Amy looked down at her feet, truly surprised to see only navy blue socks covering them. "I'm a mess," she declared before turning to head back to her bedroom. "You'd think I was getting ready for my first date ever. This is ridiculous!"

Brenda smiled as she went back to frying chicken. The sound of a car engine caught her attention, and she looked out the kitchen window to see Joel emerge from his car and move toward the lighted workshop where Neil was working.

Amy rushed to the window a few seconds later. "Is he here?"

"He's out talking to your dad. He'll be here in a minute."

Amy stepped back and nervously rubbed her hands down the length of her sweater. "Are you sure I look okay?"

"Those shoes make the outfit," Brenda teased.

Amy looked down with a horrified expression, fully expecting some strange combination of shoes to be on her feet.

"I'm only kidding!" Brenda patted her daughter's shoulder. "Calm down."

"You're right." Amy took a deep breath. "I'm being silly. Joel is no big deal."

The sound of the back door opening had her whirling around. Joel stood within its arch, his eyes going to and instantly holding hers. He, too, was dressed in jeans and a thick black sweater that seemed to emphasize his fair hair and eyes.

"Hi," he said finally, softly.

"Hi." She started to back toward the hallway. "Let me get my purse, and I'll be ready."

Amy disappeared from the room, and Brenda walked over to stand in front of Joel. She lifted her hand and slowly moved it back and forth in front of his face.

"Are you in there?" she asked playfully.

A sheepish grin split his face. "Brenda, I feel like a sixteen-year-old on his first date. It's crazy."

Brenda patted his shoulder affectionately. "Love is in the air," she sighed.

Amy reappeared. "I'm all ready."

"Have fun, you two." Brenda looked at her daughter. "Take your key. I'm not waiting up."

"I've got it." She kissed her mother's cheek. "See you later."

It was just after ten when the movie let out. Amy and Joel emerged from the theater into the cool night air, each having thoroughly enjoyed the light comedy.

The parking lot had been full earlier, and they'd had to park in a far-off corner. Joel slid an arm around her shoulders as they walked toward the car now sitting all by itself.

Amy snuggled against his side enjoying the familiar warmth of him.

It had been an evening full of laughter and lighthearted talk. Each had purposely avoided any discussion of the deeper emotions swirling just below the surface. For a little while they wanted to be carefree, unhindered by their past mistakes and problems.

"Where to now?" Joel asked after sliding into the car and starting the engine.

Amy checked her watch. "It's after ten. I suppose we'd better call it an evening."

"Ah, come on," he complained. "It's still early. How about a cup of coffee and a piece of pie?"

"I have to get up at six."

"Hot apple pie with a dip of ice cream?" he coaxed.

Amy groaned. "That's not fair and you know it."

"You're right. I'll take you home."

"Take me to Pies and Things."

"Whatever you say."

She could hear the smile in his voice and reached over to smack his arm. In a quick move, he caught her hand and brought it to his mouth to press a kiss to her palm.

Their eyes met and held. She moved to pull away, but his grip tightened. His tongue began to trace a delicate pattern on the sensitive skin. With a shaky sigh, her eyes closed and desire coursed slowly through every inch of her responsive body. Every nerve ending was alive and just waiting for his touch or caress. She surrendered readily to his sensuous teasing.

He lowered her hand to his leg. She could feel the taut muscles of his thigh beneath the jeans and slowly inched her fingers inward.

She heard his sharp intake of breath and opened her eyes lazily. His gaze was fever bright as he watched her. Her fingers inched upward until they found their mark. She caressed him boldly, feeling the heated response through the thick denim.

Joel reached for her, dragging her as close as the gearshift would allow. When his mouth closed over hers, urgent and demanding, she held nothing back. Her unbridled response didn't disappoint. He wanted desperately just to sink into her and assuage the ache that had penetrated to his soul. But some small part of his mind had managed to stay detached and was now reminding him that this was neither the time nor the place.

He drew away slowly, pulling in air and trying to think clearly. "Amy," he whispered.

"Yes." Her hand came up to caress his cheek before sliding behind his head to urge him back to her.

"No." He pushed back into his seat.

"Oh, God," Amy moaned after a moment, running a hand over her face. "We're making out in a parking lot like a couple of love-starved teenagers."

Joel began to chuckle and reached for the defrost button on the heater. "We've steamed up the windows."

"Oh, I'm so embarrassed! Joel, what's wrong with us?"

He looked at her and laughed outright. "Honey, there isn't a thing wrong with either of us. We just need to choose our location a little better the next time."

He put the car into gear and pulled out of the parking spot. "Let's go get that pie. With lots of cold ice cream!"

Ten

On Thursday evening Joel arrived home shortly after six and felt a jolt of pleasure sear through him. Amy's car was parked in the driveway. He pulled into the garage and killed the engine. Taking a moment, he mentally prepared himself. He couldn't mess this up.

When he finally stepped into the kitchen, the scent of something cooking permeated the air. He lifted the lid on a pot and breathed deeply of the simmering beef stew. He replaced the cover and called her name softly.

When he didn't receive an answer, he went in search of her. He found her sitting on the floor of the nursery, Muffins curled beside her.

She lifted liquid amber eyes to his, and he was sure he'd made a mistake by not changing the wallpaper. He crossed to her and crouched down. "I'm sorry," he whispered, his hand reaching out to touch her cheek. "I'll change the paper tomorrow."

She shook her head. "No. I'm glad you didn't change it." She looked at the sleeping angels with gentle smiles on their faces. "Looking at this paper, I thought—Our baby is an angel now."

Emotion flooded his senses, and he found himself unable to respond with words. He reached for her and drew her into the shelter of his arms as he sat back on the carpeting. He held her, her head cradled on his shoulder, as the shadows lengthened in the room and darkness settled in.

* * *

Joel pushed his plate aside and looked across the table to Amy. "You're a good cook," he complimented.

"Between my mother and yours, I learned all kinds of cooking tricks."

"Susan didn't."

Amy shook her head. "No, she didn't. But then, she didn't really want to."

"She called me earlier at the office. She and Brad are going down to Brown County on Saturday and thought we might want to go."

Amy stood and began to clear the table. "Do you want to?"

He caught her wrist and stood. "What I want," he said softly, taking the plates from her hands, "is for us to sit down and talk for a while. Let's leave these for later."

They went into the great-room and sat down on the sofa. Muffins immediately left her perch on the back of the chair and jumped up into Amy's lap.

Joel smiled wryly. "I think Muffins missed you. But not half as much as I did." He waited for Amy to meet his gaze. "I think it's time to decide where we go from here, Amy. You have to tell me what you want."

"I want to start all over," she answered without hesitation. "We got everything so turned around and messed up. Can't we try to go back and do it right?"

"We can," he said slowly. "But the fact remains that we are married. What do you want to do about that?"

"I don't want to change it."

"Good. I don't either." He hesitated, watching her. "Will you come back home?"

She looked at him a long, thoughtful moment, then shook her head. "I still need some time. I'm not ready to make that total commitment yet."

Joel couldn't help the quick stab of regret he felt. But it

was tempered by the fact that she was here now, and she did want to make their relationship work. He smiled gently. "We wouldn't really be starting over if we started at that point, would we?"

Amy felt a rush of love swell up inside. He loved her enough to let her set the pace. "Thank you for giving me time to work things out."

He tenderly cupped her cheek in the palm of his hand. "I love you, Amy. I want you to be happy. When you come home to me, I want it to be because you want to be here. No other reason will do."

She smiled at him, loving him with her eyes. "Let's go to Brown County on Saturday."

"You got it," he promised.

Amy hadn't been to Brown County State Park since she'd graduated from college, but she hadn't forgotten how spectacular it was at this time of year. Trees dressed in multi-colored leaves could be viewed from different vantage points throughout the park. A sea of orange, yellow, and red flowed in all directions.

After a morning of sightseeing and some shopping, Susan announced that lunch was definitely in order. They decided on a restaurant known for its rustic architecture and old-fashioned decor, not to mention some of the best home-style cooking around.

They were seated next to a window that gave a breathtaking view of the colorful woods beyond the glass. Susan settled into the chair Brad held for her. "I'm exhausted. This business of walking for two isn't very fair."

Brad sat beside her and chuckled softly. "I thought maybe it was the shopping for two that was tiring you out."

"I haven't bought that much," she protested.

"Brad's going to have to take a second job if you don't slow down," Joel predicted playfully.

She responded by sticking her tongue out at him with all the aplomb of a six-year-old.

Amy shook her head. "You two are hopeless. Now behave yourselves and decide what you're going to order."

"Fried chicken," Susan answered. "It's the best."

"And the deep-fried biscuits smothered with homemade apple butter," Amy added. "Remember how good those were?"

The waitress stepped up to the table to take their requests. Four orders of fried chicken with all the trimmings, including deep-fried biscuits, were ordered.

Susan leaned back in her chair after the waitress departed and stretched her legs out. She gasped softly and placed a hand on her steadily expanding stomach.

"What is it?" Amy sat forward, concern etched on her features.

"It's okay," Susan assured her as she reached for her hand. "Here." She positioned Amy's hand on her stomach. "You can feel the baby move."

Amy waited, barely breathing. After a moment she felt the faintest of movement, almost as if a butterfly had brushed its wings against her palm. She looked at Susan, and a slow smile curved her mouth. "What a fantastic feeling."

"I love it. It's so special knowing that he's alive and moving around in there."

Joel watched the two women with tender curiosity. Again, he was amazed at the bond that existed between his sister and his wife. She could easily have resented the life growing inside her friend, but Amy welcomed the opportunity to share Susan's happiness.

"Susan nearly scared me to death the first time the baby moved," Brad said. "I was asleep, and she suddenly grabbed my arm. I jerked up and looked at her, and tears were just rolling down her cheeks. I thought something was wrong." He stopped, his embarrassed gaze flying to Amy.

"It's okay," she assured him gently.

"Anyway," Susan inserted, picking up the story. "I was just so moved by the whole experience. Raging hormones, I guess. I'm either crying buckets or laughing hysterically."

Amy felt a warmth envelop her hand and looked down to see Joel's fingers enfold hers. Without words being spoken, she was aware of how very much she was loved by this man.

Amy examined the morning star quilt, impressed with the quality of the workmanship. Someone had obviously spent a good deal of time creating this beautiful and practical work of art.

She had always longed to learn how to quilt. Unfortunately, it was one thing that neither her mother nor Anne knew anything about. She promised herself that one day she would take the time to learn.

Two strong hands came to rest on her shoulders. Without turning to look she knew it was Joel. She leaned back against the hard lines of his body. The slight movement sent a thrill of pleasure coursing through him. He bent forward and kissed her cheek.

"Have I told you that I think you're a fantastic lady?"

His low-pitched voice caused a tingling sensation along her spine. She turned and eyed him curiously. "And what did I do to earn such high praise?"

His hands came back again to rest on her shoulders. "The way you handle yourself. The way you haven't allowed your tragedy to affect your relationship with Susan."

"I could never hurt her that way. She means too much to me."

"You have no idea how special you are."

"I'm not special." She shrugged. "I'm just me. That's the way I am."

"Well, you're special to me." He brushed her cheek with

the back of his fingers. "What were you looking at when I walked up?"

She turned and lifted the corner of the quilt. "It's so beautiful, but the price is a little too steep for my budget. I'm going to learn how to quilt so I can make my own."

Joel touched the blue calico fabric. "Looks like a lot of work went into this."

"I'm sure it did." Amy turned when she heard Susan call her name.

"She's off and running again," she said ruefully. "I better go see what she's found this time."

Joel watched Amy wind her way through the shop toward where she'd last seen Susan. Without a moment's hesitation he turned and picked up the quilt. He carried it to the cashier, unconcerned by the price. The quilt would go on *their* bed.

"Do you think Joel will be surprised?" Susan asked.

Amy shook her head. "I doubt it. Your mother doesn't lie well."

"Well, of course she doesn't," Susan said. "It's not in her nature."

"It doesn't matter." Amy lifted the lid on a covered dish and breathed in the aroma of the baked macaroni and cheese. "She'll get him here one way or another."

Both women turned at the sound of flames licking through the huge pile of brush and wood behind them.

"Well, that ought to roast a few hot dogs and marshmallows," Brad commented as he brushed his hands on his jeans. "Here comes someone now."

Amy turned to look as headlights came into view up the rutted lane. She'd worried about giving directions to the field at the back of her father's land. Finally, she'd told everyone to just look for the bonfire.

It was Joel's birthday, and she and Susan had cooked up this idea of surprising him with a weiner roast complete with an old-fashioned hayride. They couldn't have asked for better weather. Warm Indian summer air had settled over the area a few days earlier, and the late October night was mild. The sky was clear, scattered with stars and a moon on the back side of full.

She held her watch up toward the light cast from a nearby kerosene lantern and saw that it was just after seven. Joel was supposed to arrive by seven-thirty, if his mother could get him out here.

Within ten minutes, the crowd around the bonfire had grown from three to fifteen. The two makeshift tables were covered with a variety of food and soft drinks, as well as a birthday cake sporting thirty-three candles. Sitting off to the side were the sticks Neil had sharpened for the sole purpose of roasting hot dogs and marshmallows. The fire had died down and was just about right for cooking.

"He's late," Susan announced, coming up beside Amy. "What if he doesn't show up?"

"Then I guess I won't have anyone to cuddle up with on the hayride." Amy smiled at her sister-in-law. "He'll be here, even if Anne has to tell him why he's coming all the way out here."

"Oh." Susan sounded disappointed as she reached for a potato chip. "I hope she doesn't have to do that. I really want to surprise him."

Joel was tired and more than a little irritated. He had just gotten home from work when his mother had called. First, she wished him a happy birthday. Then she told him the water heater seemed to be leaking and asked if he could come look at it. Not exactly what he wanted to be doing on his birthday.

What he wanted to do was see Amy. He was tired of this waiting game she was playing.

They'd spent nearly every evening together for the last

few weeks. He loved being with her, and he knew she was enjoying it, too. He felt ridiculous going home alone when they had every right to go home together and be together— intimately. Just the thought of it made him restless. The chemistry between them was a powerful and heady force. And he knew she felt it as strongly as he did.

Dr. Rowland had given her a clean bill of health. Physically, there was nothing to keep them from being together. Yet she insisted she wasn't ready.

He hadn't seen or spoken to her in the last two days. She hadn't even called to wish him a happy birthday. He'd never admit it out loud, but he'd been waiting all day long for her to call. He'd even expected her to be at the house when he got home. So much for wishful thinking.

"Stupid," he muttered to himself as he pulled into his mother's driveway.

Anne was waiting on the porch when Joel climbed out of the car. He looked toward the Michaels' house, saw it was dark, then turned to his mother. "Do you know where Amy is?"

Anne looked slightly surprised before shaking her head. "I haven't seen her today. Why?"

He shrugged and came around the front of the car. "Just wondering."

"Before you look at the water heater, I think there's something else you need to check on."

Joel took a deep breath and let it out slowly. "What is it?"

"Well, Neil got a call a few minutes ago from Ed Brown on the back road. He says it looks like a group of teenagers have decided to have a keg party in the back field. They've got a bonfire going and—"

"Damn!" Joel swung around and headed back toward the car. "Did Neil go out there by himself? Did he call the sheriff?"

"No, I don't think so."

"How long ago did he leave?"

Anne shrugged. "About ten minutes ago."

"Call the sheriff," Joel instructed as he jerked open the car door and slid in.

"Yes, dear," she answered sweetly.

Joel maneuvered the dark country roads with ease and arrived at the unmarked lane within five minutes. He could see the glow from the bonfire and swore softly.

Several cars were parked off to the side, close to Ed's hay wagon. A fire blazed and tables were set up close by. But there was no one in sight.

When his headlights caught the reflection of Amy's car, he pulled in behind it and cut the engine. What the hell was she doing out here? He got out and walked slowly toward the lighted area. He was approaching the wagon and stopped in his tracks when Amy stepped out from behind it.

"Hi!" she greeted brightly.

"What's going on?"

She moved closer to him. "Nothing." Her voice dropped to a seductive note, and she smiled up at him. "Yet." She reached out and ran her hand up his chest. "I'm glad you're here."

He watched her warily but didn't respond as she slid her arms upward to curve around his neck. Her scent came with her and surrounded him in an invisible mist, affecting his ability to think clearly. Automatically, his hands came up to encase her waist, gently urging her closer.

It didn't seem important just then that they were standing in the middle of nowhere and he didn't know why. Nothing mattered but the fact that her lips were a mere inch from his, and he was desperate to taste their sweetness. His head lowered, his eyes closed, and his breath caught in anticipation.

"Happy birthday!" The shout of voices that rose from the wagon bed were more effective that an ice cold bucket of water would have been at that particular moment. Joel jerked away from Amy and stared in confusion at the familiar group happily singing off-key.

"Happy birthday, Joel," Susan said as Brad easily lifted her down from the wagon. "Are you surprised?"

His eyes narrowed. "You had Mom lie just to do this to me?"

"That's right!" She reached up and kissed his cheek. "She did a great job, too! You were really surprised, weren't you."

"You got me. I was definitely not expecting this."

Someone called Susan's name, and she turned away. Brad clasped his brother-in-law by the shoulder and drew him away a few steps. "Sorry to interrupt the moment like that," he offered softly, casting a glance to Amy. "I'd be mad as hell if I were you."

Joel's gaze flicked to Amy briefly before he nodded, and a wicked gleam came into his eyes. "Don't worry about it, Brad. I'll get even."

"Come on, Brad." Susan tugged on his sweatshirt. "You can roast me a hot dog."

It was nearly ten minutes later before Joel found himself free to talk to Amy. The group had all drifted toward the fire and were now busy roasting hot dogs. Voices and laughter carried on the still night air.

Joel slid his hands into the pockets of his jeans and waited a full minute before turning to look at his wife. Warily, she watched as he slowly walked toward her.

"You set me up," he said, his voice low and smooth.

"Guilty." She began to giggle. "The expression on your face was priceless."

He nodded. "I'm sure it was." He stepped closer to her, the heat from his body reaching out to her. "Finish what you started. Just like you started it."

Her brows rose in surprise. "That sounds like an order."

"It is." The challenge was clear in his eyes.

Her pulse reacted violently, but she didn't hesitate. "I'm

glad you're here," she said softly, her arms sliding again around his neck. "I've been waiting for you."

Joel forced himself to keep his hands in his pockets. Amy stepped closer. Her hand cupped the back of his neck and slid up into his hair, gently urging his head down. Her mouth was so warm, so persuasive, that it nearly destroyed his plans for revenge.

It took every ounce of willpower he possessed not to drag her into his arms and thoroughly plunder the soft and willing lips. But he held on and after a moment, she drew back, and looked up at him with questioning eyes.

"Thanks." He turned and started toward the bonfire. After a few steps he stopped and looked back at her, enjoying the stunned expression on her face. "Come on. It's my birthday. You can roast my hot dog."

He didn't try to hide his grin as he turned away.

Amy had the distinct impression that Joel was playing some kind of mind game with her. Her gaze went to his profile across the bonfire, where he was involved in a conversation with another couple. If he was aware of her presence, he didn't show it.

"Your marshmallow is on fire." Brad dropped onto the bench beside her.

Amy jerked the stick upward, and waved the flaming, gooey mess into the air. She blew the fire out and let the blackened confection plop to the ground.

"Here." Brad took the stick from her and withdrew two fresh marshmallows from the bag beside her. "Let me show you how it's done."

"Thanks."

He found a pocket of glowing embers to gently toast the marshmallows. "So. Do you think everyone is having a good time?"

Amy shrugged. "Looks like."

"What about you?"

She looked at him. "Joel's acting a little strange, don't you think?"

He studied his brother-in-law. "Looks like he's having a good time to me."

"He's ignoring me for some reason. I don't know if he's mad or what."

Brad carefully rotated the stick to ensure even cooking. "Well, he won't be able to ignore you on the hayride, will he? Everybody is a matched set, so that leaves you two to each other."

"I guess."

"Here you go." Brad withdrew the stick from the fire, two perfectly toasted marshmallows on the end of it. "Golden brown on the outside, gooey on the inside."

"Those are mine, aren't they?"

Amy hadn't noticed Joel come around the fire to her. He settled beside her and nodded toward the stick in her hand. "At least share with me?"

"I'll leave you two to fight it out," Brad said, rising.

Amy noticed they were now all alone beside the fire. Everyone seemed to have drifted toward the wagon, awaiting the arrival of Ed Brown to drive the tractor for the hayride.

"This is fun," Joel said as he reached for the stick. "Was it your idea?"

"Mine and Susan's."

"Two great minds," he murmured. He slid one marshmallow off the stick and turned to her. "Want it?"

She looked into his eyes, mesmerized by the glow of the fire in his blue eyes—and something else. Something dark and edgy and mysterious. He brought the marshmallow to her mouth, and her lips parted automatically to take it from his fingers.

She didn't even take her eyes from his when she reached for the stick and removed the other marshmallow. She extended it to him, and his lips closed around it. When she went to draw her hand away, he unexpectedly caught her wrist. He brought it back to his mouth and gently, one by one, sucked the sticky sweetness from her fingers.

Amy's breath stopped as a piercing response to his sensuous lips shot through her body. He'd managed to create a fire within her as hot as the one they sat beside. The world had disappeared around them. There was only Joel, and the fantastic fireworks going off inside her body. He was all that mattered, all that would ever matter.

He matched his hand to hers and entwined their fingers. Lifting his other hand, he gently slid his fingers into her hair. Instinctively, she tilted her head, encouraging the gift of his caress. Her eyes closed as contentment and desire swept through her.

"Open your eyes." His voice came to her like a whisper wrapped in satin. She responded and boldly met his clear, blue gaze.

"Do you love me, Amy?"

His question somehow managed to penetrate the thick fog swirling through her brain, and she nodded.

"Come home with me tonight."

The fog began to clear with his words. She wanted to say yes without reservations.

"Come on, you two! The hayride is leaving."

The intruding voice seemed to come to Amy from somewhere far away. For a moment, the words didn't even register. Then, somehow, her brain made the connection that Joel was standing and pulling her to her feet. She swayed slightly, and he reached out to steady her.

"Are you okay?"

She looked up into his face. He appeared calm, but she could hear his ragged breathing. "I'm not sure," she admitted.

"Don't you think it's time you came home, and we quit playing these games?"

"I don't know." She shook her head. "I can't think straight when I'm with you like this."

"That's the problem, Amy. You think too damn much. You know we belong together. Your body tells you so every time I'm near you. Why are you making it so difficult?"

"I need to be sure what we feel is real."

"What you just felt didn't seem real?"

"That's just sexual. Our feelings have to go deeper than that."

"I don't know if my feelings can go any deeper. I felt like someone ripped my heart out when I found you lying in the hallway that morning. I feel like I've been living half a life since you've been gone the last few weeks. How much deeper do my feelings need to go?"

"I don't know!" she cried, confused by the sudden intensity of his questions.

"I love you, Amy. It doesn't get any more complicated or any simpler than that. Think about it." He turned and started for the wagon, leaving her to follow on her own.

Eleven

The party began to break up after midnight. A half hour later the only thing left to do was make sure the fire was out. Joel turned to Brad. "You and Susan go on home. I'll take care of this."

"Okay. Susan's exhausted."

Goodnights were exchanged as Amy put the last of the leftovers into her car. She watched the taillights of Brad and Susan's car disappeared down the lane.

Joel was busy shoveling dirt onto the fire, and she hesitated to approach him. He wasn't very happy with her right now, and she didn't have the answers he wanted to hear.

With a sigh of resignation, she walked toward him.

"Do you have everything?" Joel asked when she stopped a few feet away.

"Yeah. It's all in the car."

"I think that'll do it then," he said, making sure the fire was thoroughly banked. "I'll get the lantern for you."

She walked back to her car. Within seconds the field was dark, with only the moon and stars for light. She opened the trunk and waited for Joel to bring the shovel and lantern.

"Thanks for your help," she said.

"Thanks for the party. It was fun."

Her eyes were adjusting to the darkness, and she could see his shadowed face clearly.

Slowly, he moved closer until she was sandwiched between the heat of his body and the cool metal of her car. His hands came up to frame her face.

"You know what I'd really like for my birthday?" he whispered as he bent toward her. "This." His lips brushed her cheek. "And this." He gently kissed her neck and nuzzled the sensitive skin just above her sweater. "And this." She barely had time to think before his mouth found hers, stealing her breath and drawing a quick and heated response.

Amy's arms slid around his waist, her fingers pressing into his back, urging him closer. He obliged, resting the length of his body against hers, hard lines to soft contours. She wanted his touch now more than she wanted her next breath. All logic and reason were gone, replaced by wants and desires and needs.

His mouth became ruthless, demanding more from her. She met his demands eagerly, opening to him, pulling him closer with quick, impatient hands.

He released the clasp of her bra and claimed for his own the tender flesh beneath the silky material. Pure pleasure raced through her, creating sensations that left her breathless.

There was no resistance when Joel pulled the sweater over her head. Her bra went next, replaced instantly by the heat of his mouth on her breast. Her hand held him to her, greedily guiding his movements. Her cry of pleasure echoed in the still night.

With a ragged breath, Joel pulled her against his solid frame, leaving no secret of his desire for her. His hands spanned her naked back, and his heart pounded frantically beneath her palm.

He looked down into her face. "It's your call, Amy." His voice was strained and hard.

She straightened and tried to push away from him.

His arms tightened, and he held her a moment longer, raw passion flaming in his eyes. Then abruptly, he dropped his arms and stepped back. Reaching around her, he retrieved her discarded sweater from the bumper of the car and handed it to her. Silently, he turned away.

Amy's hands were trembling so badly she could barely manage to get the sweater on. Her body was still on fire, clamoring for any kind of release. She was almost certain it was going to come in the form of tears.

She looked at Joel's stiff back and smoothed the sweater down over her hips. "I . . ." Her voice broke, and she swallowed hard. "I need to go. I'm tired."

He turned to her. "You're not tired. You want to go to bed with me, and we both know it. Hell, we could be making love right now in the back of that hay wagon." His voice had dropped to a husky whisper. "Right now I could kiss you and touch you in just the right way, and the only thing in the world that would matter would be making love."

She looked away from him, unable to argue. She'd be a fool and a liar to deny the power he held over her.

He slid his hands into his pockets. "I'm not going to make it that easy for you," he said, after a moment. "You've chosen the rules of this game we're playing, so you're going to have to be the one to change them. You know how I feel about you. When you're sure about your own feelings, then come and see me."

She stared at him as he turned and started for his car. "Wait a minute," she demanded. "What exactly are you saying?"

He faced her. "I'm saying, simply, that I don't want to see you again until you're ready to be my wife. Completely."

She couldn't believe what she was hearing. "Is that an ultimatum?"

He considered a moment, then shrugged. "I guess you could call it that. I'm tired of the game, Amy. I want you in my life full time. Or not at all."

"What if I decide I don't want to stay married to you?" She tossed the challenge out, mentally bracing herself for his response.

He grew very still. He lifted his eyes to meet hers. "Then I suspect that I'll be a very lonely man because you're the only woman I'm going to love in this lifetime."

With that, he climbed into his car and started the engine. She stood alone in the field, watching the taillights of his car blur and fade as tears traced down her cheeks.

"This is the most idiotic thing I can ever remember you doing." Susan's scathing tone instantly grated on Joel's nerves. He'd questioned the wisdom of his ultimatum to Amy plenty of times since the party two weeks ago. He didn't need his sister to drive the point home quite so bluntly.

"I thought you invited me for dinner." He dropped onto the sofa and stretched his legs out to rest on the coffee table.

"I did. And I wanted to talk some sense into you."

"Save your breath. There's nothing to be said."

Susan braced her hands on her hips and glared hard at him. "What the hell is wrong with you, Joel?"

That got his attention. Susan never swore. He looked at her and noticed the flush on her cheeks. "Look," he soothed, "take it easy. Don't get all worked up about this."

"It's too late. I'm already worked up. I just don't understand what you're trying to do."

"It's really none of your business. This is between Amy and me."

"You don't know how upset she is."

He gave a short, humorless laugh. "She can't be that upset. She hasn't called."

"Did you really expect her to? She's got her pride. She's not going to come running to you."

Joel sat forward, his eyes narrowed. "But I have to run after her. That's fair."

"Nobody ever said it was fair." Susan walked over and dropped down onto the opposite end of the sofa from Joel.

"I just don't understand you two. It's obvious that you belong together."

"If it's so obvious, why doesn't she see it?"

Susan shook her head. "She's just scared."

"I know she's scared. She won't let me near her."

"You really love her, don't you?"

"More than anyone knows," he said softly. "But how do I convince her?"

She shrugged helplessly. "I don't know."

"Talk to her. Ambush her like you did me. Tell her what a great guy I am."

Susan laughed. "She'll just tell me to mind my own business."

"When have you ever let that stop you?"

She smacked his shoulder and stood. "Okay. I'll see what I can do."

"Thanks. You're a great sister."

"Yeah, right." Her tone revealed her skepticism. "We'll see if you feel the same way after you eat the dinner I cooked."

"You cooked?"

"Well, I knew Brad was going to be late, so I went ahead and fixed something. He'll be surprised."

She disappeared into the kitchen, and Joel shuddered at the thought of what Susan could be concocting in the kitchen.

"Well, I followed the recipe exactly. I just don't understand what went wrong." Susan kicked her shoes off and tucked her feet up under her legs before settling back into the thick cushions of Amy's sofa.

"Maybe chicken velvet soup was too complicated. It has more than two ingredients," Amy said.

"But I followed the instructions exactly." A frown wrinkled her forehead. "Doesn't it seem odd to you that I can easily program a computer to do a series of complicated mathematical equations, but I can't follow a simple recipe?"

"Maybe it would be for the good of all mankind if you just stayed out of the kitchen. Any kitchen."

"I know." Susan sighed and smoothed the bottom of her maternity top. "Joel said the same thing."

Amy felt the familiar jolt rip through her and wished she had some control over it. It was irritating that just the mention of his name could affect her this way. "He came for dinner?"

"Yeah. He may be a big jerk, but he is my brother."

Amy smiled slightly. "He's not a big jerk."

"Yes, he is! Who does he think he is giving you an ultimatum?"

Amy gazed down at her hands, noticing how bare her left hand looked without the simple gold band. She'd taken it off after the party and tucked it away in her jewelry box, fully intending never to wear it again. It was funny how often she'd missed it in the last three weeks. Almost as much as she missed the man who had given it to her.

"Will you be looking for your own place soon?"

Amy looked across at her friend and frowned. "What?"

"Well, since you and Joel have pretty well called it quits you should find a place of your own." She paused. "You don't want to live with your parents, do you? Kinda awkward when you start dating again."

"Is Joel dating anyone?" The question popped out before Amy could stop it. She wanted to bite her tongue off.

"Who knows?" Susan shrugged. "There's always Debra. He can boss her around all he wants, and she'll just smile sweetly and let him. She's not like you. The girl has no pride."

"Maybe he wants someone he doesn't have to marry."

"What are you talking about?"

"He had to marry me, Susan. He didn't want to."

Susan unfolded her legs and leaned forward. "Is that the real problem? You *had* to get married." Her emphasis was sarcastic. "So what? When you celebrate your golden anniversary, who will care?"

"I will."

"Did he force you?"

"What?" Amy was stunned by the question.

"Did Joel force you into bed that night?"

"No, of course not."

"Then stop making it sound like he did. You were a willing participant."

"You don't understand."

"You're right, I don't. But I'm going to have my say now and then I'm not going to discuss this whole ridiculous matter again with either you or Joel." She took a deep steadying breath and stared hard at Amy. "My personal opinion is that you are a coward. You're afraid to take a chance with Joel."

"I don't remember asking for your opinion," Amy returned coldly.

"You didn't, but you got it anyway." Susan reached for her shoes. "I'm getting out of here. I don't need this aggravation."

"He acted like our night together meant nothing. He turned his back on me."

"Wait a minute." Susan pinned Amy with angry blue eyes. "He didn't turn his back on you. From the moment he knew you were pregnant, he was there for you."

"Out of obligation."

"Out of love." Susan pushed to her feet.

"But I had to come to him. He didn't call me."

"He was confused. Weren't you?"

"I was in love."

"So was he. He just didn't know it at the time."

Amy rose to face her lifelong friend.

"Amy, make a decision. If you're going to call it quits, then go ahead and do it. Get on with your life and let Joel get on with his."

"And if I do, does that mean our friendship is over, too?"

"I love Joel. He's my brother. And I love you. That won't change, no matter what happens." She bent and picked up her coat. "I'll see you later."

Amy didn't move or speak; she only listened to the sound of Susan leaving.

Amy watched the swirling snowflakes from the kitchen window as she washed the last of the Thanksgiving dinner dishes. There weren't many. It had been just her parents and herself. This had been the first year she could remember that they hadn't shared the big meal with the Hartmans.

She sighed as she rinsed the last of the soapsuds down the drain. She missed them all. She hadn't talked to Susan since their conversation last week. Had Joel invited someone to Susan's to share their Thanksgiving dinner? The unexpected thought brought with it a surge of fresh pain.

She missed Joel. She missed his voice, his smile, his touch, his presence. She missed being a part of his life.

It was probably time she faced the truth.

Reaching for the towel, she dried her hands and checked the time. She wondered if Joel would be home from Susan's by now.

Joel blessed the genius who had invented the remote control. He could control fifty-three cable stations with just the flick of his finger, but he couldn't find a John Wayne movie to save his life.

The mantel clock chimed eight o'clock. He stopped at the weather station and listened to a winter storm warning. Six to ten inches of snow. Subzero temperatures and brisk winds. He was glad he wasn't planning to go anywhere.

He tossed the remote onto the coffee table and walked into the kitchen. He retrieved a soda from the refrigerator. He popped the top and took a long drink, then leaned against the counter to ponder his messed-up life.

He'd pushed Amy away. He should have known better. His ultimatum had been a stupid ploy to get her to admit that she loved him. And like everything else he'd tried with Amy, it had failed miserably.

He took a deep breath and silently toasted himself. "Hartman, you're a first class jerk. Again."

Thanksgiving dinner today at Susan's had felt all wrong. Amy and her parents should have been there. They belonged there. As hard as Susan tried to make it a joyful occasion, it had fallen short of the mark. There was a huge void in all their lives now, and it was his fault.

He wanted to see her. Now.

Joel walked to the window and looked out at the mounting snow. The wind made a low howling sound as it whipped the curtain of white into a frenzy. There were at least two inches on the ground now. Joel knew from years of experience how quickly snow drifted across open country roads. He'd be plain stupid to try to drive to Amy's tonight.

The phone rang behind him, and he moved to catch it on the second ring. "Hello?"

"Joel, this is Neil."

"Hi. What's up?" He'd heard the edge in Neil's voice and knew this was no social call.

"Is Amy there?"

"No. Should she be?"

"She left here over an hour ago. She said she had to see you tonight."

"You let her go in this storm?"

"Do you think I didn't try to stop her? Dammit, Joel. A mere blizzard wasn't going to stop her."

"Holy cow." Joel scooped up his car keys from the coffee table.

"I drove as far as the interstate and didn't see any sign of her. The roads are covered with ice."

"Maybe she went through town."

"I wish I knew."

"You sure she was coming here?"

"I'm positive. She said she was going home."

Joel didn't speak for a moment as the words echoed inside his head. Amy was coming home. Her timing was terrible, but her heart was in the right place.

"Don't worry, Neil. I'll find her."

"Be careful. It's bad out there."

He grabbed a couple of heavy blankets and a flashlight and left the house.

The snow was coming down fast and in a blinding curtain that the car headlights could barely penetrate. Beneath the snow was a thin sheet of dangerous ice.

He inched along the nearly deserted streets, straining to see through the whirling whiteness. He decided to head for the interstate, figuring Amy would have come that way.

With each creeping minute, Joel's anxiety grew. What if she'd had an accident? She could be in a hospital emergency room right now, and he had no way of knowing. What if she was stranded by the side of the road? Did she know to make sure the tail pipe was open so that carbon monoxide wouldn't back up into the car?

"Keep thinking those good thoughts," he muttered.

The signs marking the interstate were just ahead, and he knew it was unlikely that he could see anything on the northbound side. The snow was too thick. Unless Amy's car was sitting in the median, he knew there was little hope of spotting her.

He pulled into a gas station and reached for the car phone. He checked in with Neil, hoping that Amy had called. She hadn't. He hung up.

Carefully, he pulled out onto the street when a movement on the other side of the street caught his eye. He could just make out someone walking into the wind, hunched forward. A street light illuminated the figure briefly. Intuition told him it was Amy.

He turned the wheel sharply, fishtailing across the intersection until he was facing the opposite direction. He drew up alongside her, but she kept her head bent and continued walking. Joel threw the car into park and turned on his emergency blinkers before jumping out.

"Hey!" he yelled as he came around the front of the car.

She tried to answer, but her teeth were chattering so violently she couldn't speak. Without further consideration, he swung her up into his arms and started back to the car. Twice, he nearly lost his footing, but finally managed to get her into the warm vehicle.

He climbed in beside her and reached into the backseat for the blankets. He looked over to see her struggling with the zipper of her coat. She hadn't had gloves on, and it was obvious her fingers were nearly frozen.

"Ah, Amy." Irritation and tenderness were combined in the two brief words. He reached across to pull the zipper open and help her out of the soaked coat.

He looked at her. "You need a keeper," he stated with a sigh. "What were you thinking about to risk coming out on a night like this?"

Wide amber eyes stared back at him, clear and bright. "You," she whispered. "I love you, Joel."

A heartbeat passed, and then he was reaching for her, heating her lips with his and sharing the warmth of his body with her. He felt the shiver run through her and tightened his arms around her a moment longer.

He sat back in his own seat and pulled the safety belt tight.

She sniffled. "Sorry. I know I screwed up."

He couldn't keep a pleased grin from appearing on his face. "Yeah, big time." He reached over to cup her cheek. "But I'm not sorry you did."

He reached for the phone and punched in a number he knew by heart. "Here," he said, handing it to her. "Let your parents know you're okay." She took the phone, and Joel turned his attention back to the street. "I'll try to get us home in one piece."

Twelve

"I can walk." Amy's declaration fell on deaf ears. Joel had ordered her to stay put while he pulled off his wet boots and soggy coat. Then he gathered her, along with the blankets, into his arms and entered the house through the garage. He carried her directly to the bedroom and placed her on the bed.

"I'll run you a hot bath." He turned away, but she reached out and caught the sleeve of his blue sweater.

"I don't need a hot bath," she protested quietly. "What I need is you."

His mouth went dry, and his heart kicked over in his chest. He reached out and let his fingertips graze her cheek. "You're half frozen, Amy. You need to warm up."

Her eyes gleamed with mischief. "Okay. Warm me up. Skin on skin." She shrugged out of the blankets and then reached up to loop her arms around his neck.

A man made of stone might have stood a chance against her. Joel reached out and framed her face with his hands. Amber eyes stared back at him, clear and calm, shadow free. The love was there and the trust. He silently thanked God for this woman who believed in second chances.

She tightened her arms around his neck and pulled him down as she laid back on the bed. He braced himself on his forearms, easing the weight of his body on hers. Her fingers combed restlessly through his hair as she smiled up at him.

Amy saw pleasure and desire spark in his blue eyes, causing a liquid fire to begin a slow, steady journey through her veins. It felt glorious.

His head lowered. Her eyes closed the instant his mouth touched hers. A heartbeat later, her world disintegrated, unleashing a wild rush of passion that surged through her, to him and back again. She held him tight, needing to feel the unyielding strength of him.

Patiently, his lips teased her face and neck as his hands began a gentle exploration of her body. With infinite care he undressed her, taking time to pay homage to each inch of flesh he uncovered.

By the time he reached the final barrier, a dusty-pink lace and silk teddy, she was trembling violently.

Joel ran a hand down the length of her, enjoying the silk of the garment and the satin of her skin. He felt the tremors race through her body. "You're shivering. You must be cold."

She gave a shaky laugh and opened her eyes. "I'm about to go up in flames."

"Are you?" he murmured. He made another leisurely sweep of the silky fabric. "This little number is a surprise." He bent to press a moist kiss to the sensitive hollow between her breasts. He heard her gasp of pleasure and felt her fingers tighten in his hair. He lifted his head. "I like it."

"I was planning ahead," she managed to say.

The flare of heat that jumped into his eyes said more than words ever could. But it was the slow, wicked smile curving his mouth that had her tumbling headfirst into the flames.

Amy gave herself to him, allowing him to take her to levels of delight she had tasted only one other time. His magic had her soaring to feverish heights before letting her float like a feather back to earth again. She withstood the sweet torture time and again before her mind and body came together and demanded absolute fulfillment.

"Make love to me," she demanded.

Masculine humor danced in his eyes. "What have I been doing?"

"Torturing me."

He bent to bury his face in her neck. "And you hated every minute of it?" he murmured against her skin.

She arched her head to the side to give him better access. "Now, Joel." A sigh whispered across her lips. "Make love to me now."

He pushed away from her and lifted her hand to his lips. "My pleasure." He kissed the inside of her wrist. "In anticipation of this moment, I purchased something to prevent you from getting pregnant. However, it's in the bathroom, and I need to go and get it before we go any farther."

"My hero," she whispered, as her hands tunneled under the thick sweater he wore. The feel of muscle beneath a hair-roughened chest sent another shiver through her body.

"I'm no hero. I learn from my mistakes. I don't want you pregnant again until you're ready to be." He pulled in a sharp breath as her hand drifted downward.

She rose up on her elbow and nuzzled his neck just as he'd done to her moments before. "Take your clothes off, Joel," she murmured close to his ear. "I don't want to wait any longer."

"Amy." Her name was more of a groan than a word. "I won't put you at risk again."

"Shhh." She placed her fingertips to his lips and looked into his eyes. "It's okay. The doctor put me on birth control pills after the miscarriage. You don't have to worry about anything but making love to me." She felt her breath catch as understanding dawned in his eyes.

He eased her back onto the bed and followed her down. His lips claimed hers and once again her body was aching, begging for something only he could provide. When he

drew away moments later, she reached up with sure fingers
to pull the sweater over his head. Before he could come
back to her, she rose up to run moist, slow kisses across
his chest as her hands glided over his ribs to the waistband
of his jeans. The belt parted easily; the zipper opened with
a whisper of sound. In a bold gesture, she slid her hand
inside.

The moan that tore from Joel's lips was one of overwhelming emotion. His mind closed down to everything
but the hot sensations racing through his body. He was weak
with needs he never knew existed until this woman touched
him.

Joel floated on sexual waves of tension, trusting Amy in
a way he had never trusted anyone before. He willingly let
her manipulate and orchestrate the direction of his passion.
She touched and tasted and teased until he was sure he
would go mad from wanting.

She knelt above him. A sultry pout curved her mouth,
and he watched transfixed as her fingers slowly freed the
tiny pearl buttons down the front of the pink silk.

As each button was released he caught an enticing
glimpse of the creamy flesh beneath the soft fabric. His
breath caught in his throat when she reached up and slipped
a thin strap off her shoulder. The material dipped low, revealing the upper curve of her breast. She made an identical
movement with the other strap and instantly the silk pooled
at her waist.

Joel reached up with tender hands, easily capturing the
treasure bared for him. Amy gasped at the ripples of desire
coursing through her. She strained toward him, her head
thrown back, dark hair tumbling down her back.

A moment later, she drew away from him and stood. The
pink silk slipped to the floor at her feet. Joel rose up and
reached for her, but she pushed him back. Before he could
protest, she lowered herself to cover his body with her own.

All barriers, physical and emotional, disappeared. They

came together, months of longing seeking release, and shared equally life's ultimate pleasure.

Amy woke slowly, snuggling deeper into the thick, warm covers. She squinted at the bedside clock. It was almost noon. Surprised, her eyes opened wider and she stretched. She'd been asleep nearly fourteen hours.

She threw the covers back and slid out of bed. Joel must have retrieved her stranded car. The suitcase she had packed and left in it was now sitting inside the bedroom door. She opened it and selected the warmest socks, jeans, and sweater she had. Twenty minutes later she was showered and dressed and ready for breakfast.

She headed for the kitchen and found Joel in the great-room, bent over the coffee table, papers spread out before him. He looked up when she stopped in the doorway. "Sleeping Beauty emerges."

She enjoyed the warmth of his smile a moment. "Good thing I didn't have to work today." She moved into the kitchen and poured herself a cup of steaming coffee.

"I don't think many people are going anywhere today," he called from the other room. "We got ten inches of snow."

"I guess you managed to get my car." She walked into the great-room, the mug of coffee warming her hands.

"I had it towed. You owe me sixty bucks."

"Okay." She settled into a corner of the sofa, setting her cup on the end table.

Her hair was still damp from the shower and appeared darker than usual. It brushed her forehead and hung freely to the thick red turtleneck covering her shoulders. The flush on her cheeks was natural, and she looked rested and re-laxed.

"You'll be pleased to know I took a hot shower."

"Good. I like a clean woman. With a dirty mind."

EVERYTHING ABOUT HIM   151

"I know." She took a drink of her coffee. "Has anyone ever told you that you have an excellent bedside manner?"

He grinned. "I don't remember being beside the bed at all."

Her laughter was soft as she set the coffee aside. "Come to think of it, neither do I." She reached over to touch the back of his hand. "Thank you for taking such good care of me."

His blue eyes sobered and searched hers. "Always, Amy. What I need to know is if you'll let me."

She nodded.

He reached for her. His thumb smoothed over the bare spot on her ring finger. She read the question in his eyes.

She pushed a hand into the pocket of her jeans, fishing out the gold band. "With this ring—"

"With this ring—" He took it from her and slipped it back onto her finger. He threaded his fingers with hers and looked down at their joined hands.

"—I'm going to make damned sure you never doubt how I feel about you again."

He bent and gave her a slow, soul satisfying kiss. When he finally came up for air, Amy tilted her head back and looked up into his face.

"You know what I'd like?" Her voice was rich and warm, like honey heated by the sun.

"I know what I'd like," he returned as he concentrated on releasing the snap on her jeans.

She caught his wandering hand and brought it to her lips. "I'd like to build a snowman."

He went still, his gaze locking with hers. Laughter danced in her eyes even as she placed a heated kiss on his palm. "Are you serious?"

"It'll be fun, Joel."

"Amy. . . ."

"Oh, don't complain," she scolded as she turned and headed down the hallway. "Are there any kids in this neighborhood? Maybe we can get a snowball fight started." He could hear her rummaging around the bedroom.

He followed after her and stopped to lean in the doorway. She had already pulled on a pair of baggy sweats over her jeans and a heavy sweatshirt over the turtleneck.

"I'll go out on one condition."

She paused expectantly and looked at him. "Okay. What?"

"When we come in, you take a hot bath."

She scowled, looking every bit the rebellious ten-year-old. "Joel. . . ."

"With me."

The complaint died on her lips. "You're on."

The best gift Neil Michaels received for Christmas did not come in a brightly wrapped package. It wasn't even something he could show off or touch. His best gift was the happiness that radiated from his daughter's face as she sat on the floor with Susan, surrounded by a sea of crumpled Christmas paper.

His gaze shifted to where Joel sat across the room watching his wife. Adoration was too weak a word for what Neil saw in the younger man's eyes. He was glad that he couldn't give it a single name. A deep and abiding love consisted of many facets.

Joel felt the penetrating gaze and turned to look at his father-in-law. He had no reason to conceal his feelings. Loving Amy, and being loved by her, was the most precious gift he'd ever been given. He silently thanked the man across the room for that gift.

"Pumpkin pie is on the way," Anne called from the kitchen.

"I'm eating for two," Susan reminded her mother.

"I'll help carry," Neil offered as he rose from his chair and left the room.

Joel got up and moved over to sit in the chair behind the

two women. He reached over Susan's shoulders and patted her rounded stomach. "Are you sure you aren't eating for three?"

"Get away from me!" She slapped at his hand and missed. "Why is it that a pregnant woman becomes public property? People who wouldn't dare touch me otherwise think it's perfectly acceptable to pat my stomach."

"Maybe they're so amazed by your size they just have to touch to make sure you're real," Joel teased.

"That's mean!" Amy scolded him.

Brad looked at his brother-in-law. "You better watch what you say, Joel. She's really sensitive right now. You're going to end up making her cry."

"Oh, stop it," Susan snapped, irritated by the tears that formed so easily these days.

"See what you've done." Amy glared at her husband.

Joel leaned forward to wrap his arms around Susan's shoulders and rest his hands on her stomach. "I'm sorry," he said sincerely, dropping a kiss on her blond hair. "I was only teasing." He moved his hands, spreading his fingers apart. "Is my nephew awake?"

Susan shook her head. "He's sleeping after that huge dinner."

"Can we wake him up?" He inched his hands toward her ribs.

"No!" She caught his wrists.

"Joel, quit tormenting your sister," Anne instructed automatically as she entered the room with two plates of pie.

"Yes, Mother." He released Susan and sat back in the chair. Amy looked up at him, and he winked. She studied him a long moment and wondered what he was up to now. He looked like a man with a secret he was dying to reveal.

He took the slice of pie Anne offered him, then said casually, "Let's go for a walk after we eat this."

"You're crazy," Susan said. "I'm not going out in this weather."

"I wasn't inviting you."

"Oh," she said primly. "Good." She took a bite of her pie and glanced at Amy. "He must have been talking to you."

Amy chuckled. "I don't want to go out, either."

"It'll be worth it," he assured her.

She recognized the light in his eyes and the promise in his voice. She had no idea what he was up to, but she knew she didn't want to miss it for the world. Joel came up with the best surprises.

Amy couldn't remember many white Christmases in her lifetime. But this year it had started snowing early Christmas Eve and had continued throughout the night.

The snow still fell in a light curtain, fat, plump snowflakes floating lazily to the ground. The temperature was just below freezing, and the wind was nonexistent. The world was silent as they walked, the fresh snow untouched in the open fields around them.

Amy turned her face skyward and laughed as flakes landed on her skin. Joel caught her around the waist and brought her against his body. He bent and gently kissed the moisture from her face. Despite the layers of clothing between them, she was sure they could have easily melted the snow within a three foot radius.

Joel tossed his arm over her shoulders as they started back down the deserted road.

"Where are we going?" She snuggled deeper against him.

"We're going to check out the old Radley place."

They rounded the curve, the rundown house sitting majestically on the hilltop. "I still say that could be a beautiful house," Amy said. "All it needs is some tender loving care."

"Oh, sure," Joel scoffed. "Tearing it down is the smartest thing you could do with it."

"No. Just look at it, Joel. It could be fixed up beautifully."

He stopped at the gate and began to dig in the pocket of his leather bomber jacket. Drawing out a key, he inserted it into the padlock and opened it.

"How did you get that?" she asked incredulously as he pushed the gate open.

"I know the right people. Come on." He reached for her hand and led her up the overgrown driveway. "Watch your step. I'm not sure what's under all this snow."

They climbed the front steps, the wood strong under their feet. "See, Joel," she said. "The porch is still in good shape."

"Maybe." He dug in the same pocket, coming up with a key to open the front door.

"Well, you're just full of surprises, aren't you."

"Yep." He pushed the door open and stepped inside. Amy followed anxiously. She looked around the entryway and caught her breath.

The curved staircase leading to the top level showed dulled but solid hardwood steps. She walked to the banister and ran her hand over it.

"All it needs is some polish," she murmured, her imagination taking flight. "And these floors are gorgeous. With some buffing, this wood would gleam."

Joel watched her as she moved into the room on the left. It was a large room, with high ceilings and wide windows along the east wall, facing the road and the morning sun.

"I remember how beautiful this room was when I was here. Just imagine the sunlight streaming in first thing in the morning."

She moved on through the dining room and into the kitchen. Handcrafted oak cabinets lined one wall. "Those would have to stay," she said, biting her lip. "But the rest of this room would be a challenge."

"Why?" Joel looked at her curiously.

"Well, you'd have to update the plumbing for one thing. The wiring, too. To accommodate a dishwasher and microwave." She looked at him and smiled sadly. "A lot of work, I guess."

"Yeah. Too much," he grumbled. "Let's look upstairs."

They climbed the stairs to the upper level and found four large bedrooms and one bath. Amy stood in the middle of the largest room and looked around.

"You know what?" she said, turning to Joel. "You could use the smaller room next door as a bath and walk-in closet. It wouldn't take much work. And you'd still have three bedrooms, plus that extra room off the kitchen downstairs."

"You think putting in a modern bath up here isn't going to be tough?"

She shrugged. "I can dream, can't I? Besides, with a bath between us and the other bedrooms, we'd have some semblance of privacy when the children come along."

He walked over to slide his arms around her waist. "Exactly what are you saying, Mrs. Hartman?"

"I'm saying," she paused and reached up to kiss him, "that when I make love to you, I don't want to worry about children hovering on the other side of the wall."

He grinned, his eyes sparkling with mischief. "If you weren't so noisy . . ."

"If you didn't insist on torturing me beyond reason," she returned.

He laughed and hugged her close. "Amy, you are the light of my life. How did I go so long without knowing it?"

"You're just stubborn that way." She drew back and looked up at him. "But you're stuck now."

"Stuck isn't the word I would use." He released her and once again reached inside his coat pocket.

Amy arched her brow. "Now what? Another key?"

"Only to your heart," he murmured before handing her a jeweler's box with a green satin ribbon tied around it.

With her heart pounding, she released the bow and opened the lid of the velvet box.

"Oh, Joel," she breathed, stunned by the small treasure she held in her hands.

Her eyes sparkled as she reached out to gently touch the diamond ring. He took the box from her and removed the ring from its satin bed. Lifting her left hand, he slid the ring onto her finger. It was a perfect fit and a perfect match to the gold band she already wore.

"It's so beautiful." She stared down at her hand, then back at him. "It's exactly what I would pick for myself. How did you know?"

"You forget how well I know you."

She stepped into his arms. "Thank you," she whispered just before her lips met his. When the kiss ended, he held her close a moment, his chin resting on her head.

"So you think this house should be filled with children?" he asked quietly.

"One or two would be nice." She drew back, considering the tenderness in his eyes. "Maybe three would be good."

He released her and walked the few steps to the windows. "It would take time and a lot of hard work to fix this place up, you know." He ran his hand along the window sill.

Her pulse jumped at something in his voice, something in his manner. "I don't have trouble with hard work. Do you?"

He looked at her over his shoulder. "Not when I know it's going to make you so happy."

"Are you trying to tell me something, Joel?"

He turned to her. "The house has been inspected and was found to be structurally sound. All the things you pointed out will have to be taken care of. Plus a few others, like a new roof, insulation, and new windows, to name a few. It's going to take some money to pull it off. And we'll have twenty acres of land bordering your father's to deal with. You'd better plan on living here the rest of your life."

She shrieked and launched herself into his waiting arms.

He caught her and swung her around in a wide circle as she rained kisses over his face.

"What did I ever do to deserve you?" Tears of joy raced down her cheeks.

He set her back on her feet. "Don't you know by now that I'd do anything for you?" He wiped her tears away. "When I think of how close I came to never knowing this kind of love, I become more determined to show you how much you mean to me. Whatever the future holds, Amy, we face it together."

She smiled as she gazed up into his face, a face she had loved and trusted her whole life. She used to think she knew everything about him. Now she realized she probably never would. But it didn't matter. Judging by the promise in Joel's eyes, she'd have a lifetime to learn all she wanted to know.

COMING NEXT MONTH